# Two Hearts and Ten Roses

THE DYNAMICS OF A DYSFUNCTIONAL FAMILY

HUDENA RASHEED

outskirts press

Two Hearts and Ten Roses
The dynamics of a dysfunctional family

v1.0

This is a work of fiction. Names, characters, businesses, places, events, locales, and incidents are either the products of the author's imagination or used in a fictitious manner. Any resemblance to actual persons, living or dead, or actual events is purely coincidental.

The opinions expressed in this manuscript are solely the opinions of the author and do not represent the opinions or thoughts of the publisher. The author has represented and warranted full ownership and/or legal right to publish all the materials in this book.



Outskirts Press, Inc.
http://www.outskirtspress.com

ISBN: 978-1-9772-3446-9



PRINTED IN THE UNITED STATES OF AMERICA

I would like to thank my wife, Jacqueline, daughter Mercedes, and sons Paul, Jamaal, and Hudena Jr., along with sister Zoe, for helping me to edit this book, directly and indirectly.

I dedicate this book to my wife, children, the ten roses of my generations, family, friends, and mentors that persevered in their own lives in order to guide our paths in this life.

Also, to the past generations that have left this life and future generations that will learn from our mistakes and benefit from our triumphs in this life.

May this book give them all a better understanding of what we went through in this generation of life based on fictionally named characters and figures.

I CAN.....Always live your life with an attitude of yes, I can. The last four letters of American are "I C A N". The last four letter of Mexican are "I C A N". The last four letters of African are "I C A N".

You can do anything that you set your mind to accomplish in life. Execute your thoughts today. By the way, if you are from El Salvador, Costa Rica, Panama, Nicaragua, Belize, Honduras or Guatemala, then you are a Central American, and your last four letters are "I C A N".

I can do anything that I set my mind to accomplish in life and God will give me the strength to accomplish all my goals in life.

European Americans should say I CAN because your last 4 letters are also I CAN.

# PROLOGUE

My mom's best friend, Bertha, slowly followed me in an old grey Buick as I was walking home from school. She shouted in a stern voice, "Jump in the car because your mom is leaving your dad." My life would change forever on that one day as a little kid walking from first grade to home.

The most disheartening part of my life was when my mom and dad divorced. There is something unique about family unity and seeing them divorce was like watching a tall glass of water fall off the counter and shatter on the floor. Couples generally get over a divorce, but it has a deleterious effect on their kids.

My dad was about 5' 7" tall. He was an Army Veteran and a very handsome and charming man with curly black hair, broad shoulder, and with a rather light skin complexion. His mere presence always demanded attention. He had 5 kids with my mom, they were named Hudena, Ramona, Othello, Zoe, and Elijah. They came out of my mom's womb. for the most part, year after year in a row from 1954 to 1959.

After her last child, Elijah, my 25-year-old mom decided it was time to leave my 29-year-old dad. After my mom left him, he would spend years in depression, and the rest of his life was spent alternating between states of depression and engaging in a litany of occupations such as : preaching, working at the Long Beach Naval Shipyard, McDonnell Douglas Aircraft, auto mechanic, selling and raising plants and flowers as a horticulturist, construction work, training dogs to go to the grocery stores and bring back food and liquor, and finally raising aquarium fishes for sale.

He was indeed a bright man and a prolific reader, but he was also a deeply flawed man. He loved to tell jokes and some of the funniest jokes I have ever heard in my life came from my dad. However, he also drunk Johnny Walker Red Whiskey heavily and beat my mom with his fist until one day she finally mustered up enough courage to take her 5 kids with her and leave him.

He would later try to force her to come back to him by breaking into her project home at Imperial Court Projects in Watts. I can remember many quiet Sunday nights being disturbed by a shattering glass window in the living room. He would actually burst thru the large big plane glass window into the living room of the house. We would all run out the front door in fear that he would hurt my mom or even us and so we sought refuge over at Bertha's house. While a few of us stayed in the house sleeping, most of us ran to Bertha's house, which was always a few blocks away in the Imperial Court Projects of Watts, California. He always respected Bertha because she carried a gun and he knew better than to break into her house and her house became our place of refuge.

His continued pursuit of my mom, a beautiful housewife with long black hair, bright white teeth, lovely brown eyes, and a darker hue, would continue in vain until one day he just simply stopped.

She would later find her niche and become a store clerk and the Department Head of Produce at Kroger Grocery Store.

Robert's dad, Elijah, my grand dad, told him to let my mom, Josephine, go and to remarry and raise a new set of kids and that one day all his initial kids would come back and visit him. Later in life, he followed his dad's advice, remarried, and all his initial 5 kids would return to see him one day except for Elijah.

My dad, Robert, remarried and had four more kids, Onesimus, La Sharron, Roberta, and Rebecca with his second wife, Gloria. Years later he would die of pancreatitis and cirrhosis of the liver at the incredibly young age of 46. My mom, Josephine, would also remarry and have another kid named Ronald with my stepdad, John. Both of my parents in their respective lives would marry step parents, ironically, from the same city of Alexandria, Louisiana.

Although, I wouldn't see my actual dad for countless years, one day we would reunite and he would be instrumental in getting me into college, passing the DMV test to drive, learning how to fight against injustices, and he once even stopped me from having asthma attack. (A story that I will share later,)

He told me that some of the finest women that I would ever meet in my life attended college and that I should also attend college and marry the cream of the crop. I did indeed heed his advice.

# Chapter 1

## EARLY YEARS

I was born in 1954 during the Presidency of Dwight D. Eisenhower. Most African Americans were living under the laws of racial segregation in housing, busing, and voting rights during this time. The very next year, 1955, a courageous leader named Dr. Martin Luther King, Jr. and many others would lead the Montgomery Bus Boycott and help to bring down the walls of segregation in public transportation.

I always heard as a youngster that the main difference between down south and up north Whites was that Southern Whites said Blacks can live close to us but they can't get uppity; and the northern Whites said they can get uppity as long as they don't live close. They both practice different forms of defacto and dejure racial discrimination against people of color like me in those days.

While Dr King and others were fighting for our rights down south, my mom spent the early years of her life fighting for our economic survival after leaving my dad. She would work at the Plush Horse Restaurant in Compton, where she would meet famous actors like Frank Sinatra and Cary Grant and then she moved on to work at Compton City College fixing lunches for college students and working really hard to feed her five kids.

I can remember many days of eating Pinto Beans with ground hamburger meat and cornbread. All five of us would eat really fast so that we could be the first to get a second plate. My mom would be so excited to learn years later that while she had worked in a college kitchen as a young adult that her oldest son, Hudena, would be teaching on the college level as a professor in his later years.

While my mom was busy working, I, as a kid, was often sailing green leaves off the flowing waters that swept along the street curbs of Imperial Court in Watts, California. Other times, I was turning my mom's white sheets into marked up Superman outfits and running around the neighborhood shouting that I was Superman.

I was a young, innocent, and curious lad. I once messed with a bird's nest and the bird's mom flew toward me and struck me in the face by my right eye. A permanent mark that remains with me to this very day. I also took a water pistol and squirted water on the large flash tubes in the back of our only Black and White Television set and it never worked again. Of course, a whooping ensued for my dastardly acts.

I was always excited, at this time of my life, about the visits from our Long Beach cousins. We and our cousins would play a game called" last tag" when it was time to depart one another in those days. The memories of my Aunt Ulato and her kids coming from Long Beach to Watts to play with us in the Imperial Courts was just so much fun. We would play Hide and Seek, and other games, and the joy and laughter were simply memorable.

I also remember being a Cub Scout in those days and learning how to give directions to other scouts and learning about respect and courtesy and politeness. The quintessential Cub Scouts Motto was "Be Prepared." My mom obviously wanted me to be around other Boys and Men to learn teamwork and masculinity.

(Contrary to popular opinion, going back down memory lane can often put a smile on our face. I loved my childhood, the innocence, the outdoors, and the people who came into it were all quite fun at that time)

However, the one exception to those memories is when my babysitter, Jennifer, Bertha's daughter, molested me as a child. She played with my penis in various ways when I was a mere 5 years old. Yes, my babysitter had sex with me when I was a mere 5 years old. I was one of those kids exposed to sex at an early age. She played with my penis and put me on top of her several times while my mom was away from the house. In turn, the kids in our family were incestuous at an early age but stopped as we aged.

I would actually be 16 before I actually had consensual sex with another woman. When I was 16 years old, a girl asked me to kiss her, I kissed her on her outside lips with no tongue. Later this same girl asked me to have sex with her, but I actually didn't know anything about foreplay. I was very naïve in those days. In my later years, I would have sex with a woman and her eyes actually rolled in the back of her head like a Las Vegas Jackpot Machine win and it scared me. I now realized later that is how some women have orgasms.

(I think America is very puritanical when it comes to sex. On one hand they preach puritanical concepts, but on the other hand, they practice impurity behind closed doors. It is an undisputed fact that slaves' masters had sex with their slaves. We know this because all slaves came out with different looking shades of color, freckles, hair, and eyes. On the one hand, the church taught virtues like virginity until marriage and truth, but on the other hand they actually practice promiscuity and deceit.)

One day, our lives would change forever when my mom met John, my future stepdad. She was walking across the street in the Imperial Courts in Watts and he was in a car and whistled at her to get her attention and an inevitable romance ensued is what we were told by them.

John was a short man about 5"5" with a Napoleonic Complex that came out in forms of aggression against his own 5 step kids. He was the only child of his parents and never had the privilege of having sisters and brothers. He would tell me one day, as he and I were walking, that he may have to shoot my dad if he kept breaking in my mom's house and I immediately said to myself that I do not like this Man.

After they started dating, we abruptly left Imperial Courts and Grape Street Elementary School in Watts and moved up north to Menlo Park, California when I was in the Third grade. We lived in Menlo Park but went to school in Palo Alto. (East Palo Alto would later become the Murder Capital of America years after we left the region.) We spent about 4 years in Menlo Park, California. I attended Belle Haven Elementary School and met people like Kenneth Franklin, James Connors, and Cleo Johnson as childhood friends. We would all walk a mile to school together and talked about girls, sex, and Muhammad Ali along the way. Our parents did not like Ali's brashness, and saw him as a nonconformist, but as kids we loved him for being defiant and truthful.

One day, while in Menlo Park, my brother Othello and I climbed over our back-yard fence and broke into the neighbor's house and fixed ourselves some peanut butter and jelly sandwiches and busted open their Piggy bank. As we were leaving the house to reclimb the fence to our own backyard, my sister Ramona saw us making our getaway and said, "I am going to tell mama." I offered her money for her silence, but she refused and kept her word and told our parents. That was the end of my criminal career for a short period.

Afterwards, my mom whooped us, my stepdad whooped us, and then they asked the neighbors did they want to whoop us as well. After all those whippings, I decided that crime did not pay and went straight and started my own lawn mowing business while I was only a mere 13 years old.

In those days, we largely lived with my mom and stepdad in Menlo Park; but in the fourth grade for me and the second grade for Othello, we went to live with my Long Beach dad. We attended Roosevelt Elementary School across the street from Long Beach Poly High School. One of my best friends during this time was Brady at Roosevelt Elementary. He could fight really well and was also great at Kickball. He could actually kick the ball over the fence of Roosevelt Elementary and across the street to Poly High. The Poly High School students had to throw it back to us in order to continue the kickball game. He was considered the King of the fourth grade at that time because he could fight very well and had no challengers. I started calling myself second king because he was my best friend.

I remember one time I cut in the lunch line at school and this Mexican kid said what are you doing. I said, "I am cutting in line because I am second King of the 4th grade." He hauled off and beat my ass. He obviously did not respect my self-appointed title. Also, while we were there in the 4th grade my dad got upset that we didn't know our multiplication Tables and Roman Numerals, so he told my brother Othello and I that we could not come out of the bedroom room or eat food until we learn them. Othello and I quickly learn both subjects and still know them to this day.

Afterwards, we returned back to Menlo Park and I would end up years later at Green Oaks Jr High School. When I finally reached the middle of the 8th grade, we left Menlo Park and moved to Pontiac, Michigan. I left behind some really great friends like James, Ronnie, Cleo and Kenneth. It seemed that as soon as I developed close friendships that we would abruptly move away. I also left behind the smartest girl in class, who was

Japanese, and her name was Sandra. I liked her but she never even noticed me.

In Pontiac, Michigan I attended school at Jefferson Jr High during the remainder of my eighth-grade year. They gave various reasons for our constant moving but even at a young age, I knew it was being done to keep us away from my father. He apparently drove over 300 miles from Long Beach to Menlo Park to see us one day and this may have just upset the apple cart. Once we moved to Pontiac, Michigan, he made no more attempts to see us. He would become a distant stranger. Once my dad was out of the picture, my mom demanded that we call our stepdad John—Daddy, and of course, I objected in vain.

In Pontiac, Michigan, my stepdad, John, a Navy Veteran, got a job with Pontiac Motors. During slavery times, many Blacks worked on the plantation, but in the modern days of Pontiac, Michigan, most of them worked at the Plant is what we would say back in the days. We called the Auto Industry where GM cars were made the Plant and my stepdad was a plant worker instead of a plantation worker. An obvious dig at their title.

We initially lived in a small cramped one-bedroom house, behind a main house with 8 people in Pontiac, Michigan. My mom, stepdad and six kids. John, my stepdad would mistreat the original five kids and they, in turn, would take their anger out on my baby brother Ronald, but I always stood up for him and stopped my other brothers and sisters from beating him up. Every time I go to Pontiac, Michigan to visit, Ronald will take me out to a restaurant called Carmen's and treat me to Mexican dishes. Eventually, we moved away from the one-bedroom house to a much bigger 3-bedroom house with a basement on the Eastside of Pontiac on Elm Street. This occurred when John started doing well on the job at the Plant and my mom was hired as a Cashier at Kroger's Grocery Store.

I remember vividly on one Thanksgiving Day, my mom fixed a large Turkey dinner and we all went for a walk, as a family, before eating it. When we came back home, our dog King had eaten the entire Turkey dinner. Someone had apparently left the basement door unlocked and the dog had a field day. He looked at each of us like that Turkey dinner was good!

I recalled another time when someone tried to steal our only Chevy Impala car late at night and I heard them trying to start the engine by hot wiring the car. I was still in the eighth grade, but I impulsively ran outside and shouted, "Motherfucker get out of our car." The thief heard me and jumped out of the car and started running down the street. My stepdad John did not thank me for saving the car; instead, he chastised me for using such "foul language" and wondered where I had learned such foul language. But all I could think of was the fact that my foul language had saved the car from the thief.

The one thing I loved about Pontiac, was that it allowed me to live in snow for the first time in my life. One day my sister Ramona and I were ordered by my mom to walk to the store and buy something that she needed. It snowed profusely that day while we were walking home and became so cold that Ramona started crying. I had never seen her cry before in my life. She had always been strong, and this was the first time that I saw her vulnerability. On our way back home, a lady saw her crying and offered us a ride in her car. Ramona reluctantly got in the car while I jumped in immediately. The lady took us home while my sister was still crying due to the extreme cold. Her tears made me realize that we were no longer in sunny California and were now living in a totally different environment.

Also, while in Pontiac, I had several fights over my name. Many people could not pronounce it correctly and called me "Whodini "instead of Hudena (Hue-dee-nah). When I was little, the kids called me "Houdini "and they would tease me and tell me to do tricks. I had fights at both junior high schools of Jefferson Jr High and later at Eastern Jr. High, on the eastside of town in Pontiac. I kept demanding that they call me by my name correctly. I was always getting into fights at both schools because of my name and I would not hesitate to fight. I hated the name with a passion and hated my dad for even giving me the name. It reminded me of the Country and Western song about a boy named Sue in which a male being called Sue was always getting into fights. When he finally grows up and confronts his dad to beat him up for giving him that awful name, the dad tells him that I named you Sue to make you tough because I knew I was not going to be around in your life.

I finally stopped fighting over my name when I arrived at Long Beach Poly High School in the eleventh grade and accepted the mispronunciation. In fact, at Long Beach Poly High, people would call me "Whodidit"and 'What did it' and "Whathedoitfor" and a host of assorted and different names and I would just simply smile.

I am all grown up now. I must say I love the name because it is quite unique and different. Occasionally, a person will mispronounce it today, and I will gently make corrections by letting them know that (Hu) is for huge, and (Dena) is pronounced like Pasadena; everyone would respond with a smile!

My wife named our youngest son Hudena Junior. What is so ironic, everyone actually pronounces his name correctly; it just goes to show that this generation is totally different! I am genuinely surprised my son didn't have to go through the turmoil I went through with no explanations. I recall having to fight for people to say my name correctly and I am just sharing the memories.

I also remember at Eastern Jr High that a tall, skinny bully, named Jackie, would walk up to students in the 9th grade and demand their lunch money. Students out of fear would give him their entire lunch money. I would go home and worry and stressed over what I would do if he ever asked me. Then, one day, he asked me for my lunch money. I balled up my fists and screamed at the top of my voice, "I aint giving you shit." He looked at me like I was crazy and said, "Hudena, it is not that important", and walked away. I was so proud of myself because my fear and courage had allowed me to keep my lunch money.

I also begin to charge students to do their homework in the 9th grade at Eastern Jr High around this time and even gang-bangers would pay me to do their homework. I made a lot of money doing homework at Eastern Jr High. I was also student of the month academically. While in Pontiac, I also won a poetry contest. I also had my own paper route at that time to various homes, and I also sold Jet Magazine to neighbors. Then one day my mom got me a job at Kroger's Grocery Store as a bagboy where she worked. I was a hardworking 16-year old Kroger bag boy and making good money. I bagged the groceries, swept the floor, stock the shelves, and emptied the trash. I bought Isaac Hayes Albums and plenty of clothes, shoes, precision skates, and saved money.

One day, one of my sisters said this guy nicknamed Green Eyes was disrespecting her. He was a rather large gentleman and I confronted him and told him never to disrespect my sister again. I was shaking in my boots the whole time I was talking to him, but he never bothered her again.

I even remember my brother, Othello, being in a fight at Long Beach Poly against Larry and he was getting the better of his opponent and the opponent's friend, Elvie, said. "I am going to jump into the fight and help my buddy." I said, "If you jump in then I will jump in too!" That statement was enough to make him change his mind about joining the fight.

I even protected my cousin, Robbie, in a fight at Silverado Park in Long Beach against Arthur. He was getting the best of Robbie in the fight and I intervened to save my cousin. It was tough being a big brother and cousin in those days and I salute all big brothers and sisters that are going through it now. My advice is for you to protect your family because you are indeed the third parent.

Getting back to Pontiac, one day I asked my boss at Kroger Grocery Store why I was paid less than a coworker, who was of European Ancestry or as we colloquially call White. He was in the 12th grade and was hired after me. The boss explained to me that I indeed had seniority over him, but I was only in the 10th grade and the White guy was in the 12th grade. That explanation perplexed me since we both did the same work. I started stealing from the store and rationalizing my actions. I was again engaged in criminal activity and started taking things from the store to equalize my salary. I would throw things that I liked out of the store into the trash can and then empty the content into a big trash can behind the building outside and then go pull the stuff out of the trashcan after the store was closed. I realize it was wrong now, but at the time I was seeking revenge in a rather subtle passive aggressive manner. I felt that since I was hired before him and we were doing the same work that we should get the same pay. I had returned to my criminal ways in a passive aggressive fashion.

I would also meet Jovanna in the 10th grade in Pontiac. She was light skinned and gorgeous. Her smile often brought sunshine into the room. She was very smart, and her family was rich and rather well to do. My challenge in life was to get a kiss from one of the finest girls in the world at that time. It was like climbing the summit of Mount Everest to me. On our first and only date over Jovanna's house we played checkers for a kiss. I won the game and she kept her word and kissed me; I was so excited. It was not a French Kiss, but it was a kiss on the lips. I loved playing Checkers as a kid, but I loved a kiss as a reward even more. I heard she is married to preacher in Atlanta these days. He is so lucky to have her as a partner. A few months later, I would move to California and never see her again.

The second person I remember dating in those days was Christine. I asked her if I could walk her home from school one day at Jefferson Jr. High and she said, "Yes." As we were walking home, I asked her did she want something out of the store. She said, "No that she did not want anything." I was so happy because I did not have a penny in my pocket. I said to myself that her parents had raised her well and taught her proper manners in her saying NO. I walked her to her house several times and then one day we moved to the other side of town. I would often run from Eastern Jr High School, which would let out about 15 minutes earlier than Jefferson Jr. High, and was about two and half miles away, just to walk her home from school. Running so far to walk her home would later help me to run cross country in High School.

She would later break up with me and I actually cried like a baby. I nearly died. It seemed that life was not worth living at that time, I can remember shooting basketball on the basketball court and crying crocodile tears because she had left me. Then one day, I heard a song by Jerry Butler called, "Only the strong survive." That song really helped me to survive those dreadful days and move on in life after a very dire time in my life.

The third person I remember dating was Beverly in the 9th grade at Eastern Jr, High. Her dad owned his own Pharmacy Store in Pontiac. She was simply dark skinned and gorgeous, and she walked with pride and confidence. I tried every trick in the book to try to get her to open her legs for me, but she never would. I used upper persuasion for lower invasion but to no avail. The sweetest lines from me could not get her to spread her legs. I had memorized all the lines from the lyrics of the Temptation and Smokey Robinson Albums' and often used them on her. I heard that she is super religious these days and I think she is a minister.

Also, when I was about 16 years old, I really liked this female cashier at the Kroger Store where I worked in Bloomfield, Michigan. She was about 25 or 26 and extremely attractive. She reminded me of the Queen of Sheba. We would often sit down in the employee's lounge and discuss all types of forbidden topics at work. She knew my mom worked there and so she was very careful about what she said to me. She told me about the 69 sexual position and also how she liked men to perform cunnilingus on her. In the neighborhood we simply called it eating out. She and I would discuss a host of other forbidden topics. I finally told her one day that I really liked her a lot and she responded that she only dated Italian men. She said it was something about them that touched her soul. I was crushed to say the least. We remained friends, but this Ebony Jewel only liked Italian men. It was probably best because I was so weak behind her that I probably would of gave her my entire paycheck from Kroger. I have since met other women in my life and they too have only had a preference for one race. Some women dated only blacks and others only preferred another race like Mexicans or Asians or even European men. I guess it is simply different strokes for different folks.

I can also remember some great fights in my life at those schools that I attended, like the time Floyd beat the Bradford Brothers in Menlo Park, California in the 6th grade. He was studious and new to the school and yet he beat up both bully brothers by himself. The time also when a guy named White beat Robert at Jefferson Jr High School in Pontiac, Michigan in the 8th grade. The studious brother actually beat up the gangster.

Those were the days when men meet each other face to face and fought their differences in public and now those days are history, but they still make great memories. Some of the best fights that I ever seen in my life were not professional fights but rather after school fights.

I would have many other teenage experiences that I will share later in this book, but let's get back to my dad, whom I would not see again until I reached the 11th grade and after falling out with my stepdad. My stepdad and I fell out because I was working at Kroger Grocery Store as well as making good money and he wanted me to pay for my own schooling at Pontiac Catholic, a private school. A private school fee that I thought he and my mom should pay as they did for my other brother and sister. My stepdad also begins to open my own private mail. He said it was his house and he could open any mail that came to his house. I said, "It is your house, but you can't open up my private mail." I felt a sense of self-actualization at 16 years old as I was becoming my own unique person.

I finally left Pontiac, Michigan, because I was tired of my stepdad waking me up out of bed on Friday nights to talk to me about a woman who had left him while he was in the Navy. He was married and still drinking alcohol and remembering that she wrote him a traumatic Dear John Letter. He was reminiscing about a break-up that occurred while he was in the Navy countless years ago. He acted like it had happened yesterday. He would talk to me for hours from midnight to the early morning hours about this personal tragedy even though he was married to my mom.

I told my mom I couldn't take my stepdad anymore. We called my dad in Long Beach and he sent me a ticket to come to Long Beach. I finally moved to Long Beach to live with my real dad. The return to Long Beach allowed me to hook back up with one of my favorite cousins on the paternal side, Robbie, and we would spend many days together chasing women and partying. Robbie introduced me to Marijuana in high school and the first joint I ever smoked was at 16 with him. We even ran away from home together one day, meets some girls at the Pike (an amusement park in Long Beach) and thought we were grown, but we soon went back home when his car broke down.

I would also meet Debra at Long Beach Poly High and she would become my girlfriend for a few months and then leave me for my best friend, Olen. Her father, Hank, hired me at 16 to truck drive vending machines all over the various states of the United States. I think that was what I was hauling back in those days.

Hank was an amazing man; he was a proud and big 250-pound man with a large stomach and jovial nature. He owned his own vending machines business. He bought used vending machine, repaired them, and then resold them. He always carried loads of cash on him and could talk White businessmen out of their last penny with laughter and persuasion. One white man once told Hank that some black men rob with a gun, but you rob with your mouth. He was just that persuasive and he taught me all of his tricks. He was married to his wife Erma and she was constantly demanding that he do better in life and did everything to please her. He told me one time that he got so far behind in his house notes that he robbed a man just to pay his house note. He also told me that one-time $10,000 flew out of his car window on the highway and he put his car in reverse to go retrieve the cash. He also was an ex high school football player and he often had to strong arm people that would not pay him or his business associates. We went to Irvine one day to collect some money from this guy in a Porsche in front of a Bar and the guy pulled out a gun. I shouted, "Hank, a gun!" Hank told the guy that he would beat his ass and take away the gun. The guy put away the gun away and paid Hank the money. He was a wise man, but he also died early in life.

The move to Long Beach, however, proved to be not much better than Pontiac because my dad was now beating on my stepmom, Gloria. He was mistreating her and drinking Johnny Walker Red. My stepmom, Gloria, would cook some of the best Tacos in the world and fried Catfish like it was nobody's business. She was rather slender and had a dark hue and long hair and was exceedingly kind to me while my dad was alive. My dad simply loved dark skinned women. He always said the blacker the berry-the sweeter the juice.

My dad kept us busy at his house in Long Beach. He made my brother Othello and I do construction work on the house, feed the chickens, collect their eggs, and pick Collard Greens out of his Garden. He was an urban farmer living in a residential area on the westside of Long Beach. He also had us work on his cars by changing the oil and spark plugs and even brakes. I can remember being under those cars saying one day I will be a lawyer and pay someone to work on my cars. I found mechanical work to be arduous and mundane, but I obeyed my dad.

I eventually got tired of hearing my stepmom's screams, coming through the bedroom walls, late at night and left my dad's house in the latter part of the 12th grade. I went on to live with my first cousin, once removed, Jackie. Jackie's apartment was my place of refuge. My dad respected Jackie, she didn't tolerate mess, and he knew better than to come over her house. Then upon graduation from Long Beach Poly High School, I immediately joined the U.S Army. My brother Othello would tease me for joining the Army at that time in 1972 and told me that I was going to be killed in the Viet Nam War and why was I in the white man's Army. Two years later, he would join the Air Force. I was glad I had not listened to him.

While on the bus on the way to join the Army, I was listening to a song by Elton John called Rocket Man. The song is about an astronaut going into outer space and that is just how I felt while travelling on this new journey of my life to the unknown U.S. Army base in Fort Ord, California. Echoing in my ears also were the words of my cousin, once removed, Jackie, saying, "Aim for the Stars and if you fall short of your goals at least you would be on the moon" I would definitely heed her advice.

# Chapter 2

## TWO HEARTS

I am going to digress for a moment to talk about my marriage. My name is Hudena, I am the son of Robert and Josephine and the grandson of Elijah and Rozelle, the latter both founded St Mark's Baptist Church in Long Beach. I am also the great grandson of Wesley and Sophia on the paternal side and on the maternal side, I am the grandson of Robert and Luesther and great grandson of Queen Esther and Willie Brown on the maternal side. My predecessors, for the most part, short of Africa, hail from Little Rock, Arkansas and Elrod, Alabama.

My father, Robert, had 5 kids with my mom, Josephine, initially, and then he had 4 more with my stepmom Gloria; and my mom Josephine had one more kid with my stepdad, John, and their son was named Ronald. I call the ten of us - ten roses. In short, two hearts produced ten roses.

My wife and I are also two hearts joined passionately together and we are both the byproducts of passionate two hearts - our parents. I am now married with 4 kids, one by my first wife of a year and three by my second wife of 40 years thus far. This is simply the history of my life and my relationships from my perspective on a fictional basis.

My second wife, Jacqueline, has kept us together for these last 40 years. I tried everything I could to break us up, but she would not have it nor let me go. She finally did leave me once, but her mom, also known as Queen Esther, a beauty shop owner, told her to go back home. Her father was Robert, a light skinned African American LAPD cop, that was mistaken for a White man and shot in the Watts Riot of 1967 and yet lived to tell about it. He helped us out several times with loans in the early part of our marriage and was a financial anchor to our drifting boat in the early years of our marriage.

My first wife, my sister, and many others, tried to break up my second and current marriage to Jacqueline, but to no avail. My sister Ramona told her to leave me because I was simply no good. My ex-wife told her she saw me with another woman and even my mom told her that I was just like my dad and she should leave me. Yet, she stayed. My mom's sister, Aunt Jessie, whom I loved dearly, had a picture of my ex-wife over her house when I came to visit with my new wife, Jacqueline. I asked her to take it down. She refused. She said this was her house and she could hang up any picture that she wanted. I said I will never come over your house again. When I finally went over her house again - the picture was gone.

Women who never wanted me before suddenly became interested in me once I meant my current wife. My old wife once even sat by our bedroom window and listened to my new wife and I make love at night. The reason why I know this fact is because she told me. She called me to complain to me about making love to my new wife at the time. I can't believe she was actually listening to us make love. She would also claim to go to my dad's grave and that my dad told her that I would someday come back to her. I kept telling her we had plenty of times to get back together after we separated, and she did not want me then, and now she only wanted me because my new wife wanted me. I finally had someone in my life that did not listen to the distractions and advice of other people and that was actually committed to me and I simply refused to go back to the past.

My own mom told me I had made a mistake in marrying my second wife, Jacqueline, but I did not listen to her either and now, my mom, and my second wife cannot get enough of talking to each other these days. I am now glad I stood my ground.

The joke I often tell people about our relationship is that the police are actually looking for me because my wife called the police last night and told them that I had stolen her heart; and now I am scared to go home because I am afraid that I might get arrested for the felony of Larceny.

This second marriage is the only thing in my life that I have actually held onto for so many years. I have never kept a job more than 15 years; I have never kept a house more than 15 years; I have never kept a car more than four years. I coached track and football and basketball for 4 years and then abruptly stopped; but we have held on to this marriage continuously.

How did we meet? On October 31, 1979, I took my wife Jacqueline out for our first date. She stood me up on our first date scheduled for October 24, 1979 and simply did not show up. She then came to my office afterwards to see me; I was working at the Veteran's Affairs Office on Western State College of Law Campus. She said, "I thought you were playing about the date." I said, "I do not date woman that stand me up." She said. "Give me another chance." A week later we went out to eat at a restaurant in Long Beach and afterwards, I took her to the mountainous top of Signal Hill, near Long Beach, and I asked her to be my lady. Later that night on November 1, 1979, I asked her to be my lady and I also told her that one day I think you will be my wife. We were married 5 months later on March 31, 1980 and are now headed to our 41st Anniversary.

We have been together through thick and thin, hell and high-water, we have loss a house and bought another one; had a car repossessed and now drive three Mercedes Benzes. We have loss and gained, but we have never abandoned our marriage primarily due to my wife and that fact speaks volumes. I have cussed her out and she has cussed me out. I have told her I was leaving, and she has told me to go! She has changed me, and I have changed her. She is not the same and neither am I. Marriage is a phenomenal endeavor if you should ever be blessed to have one. There is nothing like it in the world! I don't know what the future will bring for me or her, but I do know that she has been my partner throughout my life and whatever may await us, we will be more than able to handle it with the help of our God!

I was single for about 26 years except for my brief one-year marriage to my first wife but have been married for 40 to my second wife. In short, I have been married longer than I was single, Wow! I think marriage is simply difficult. I don't think people realize just how difficult it truly is to stay married. It takes commitment, communication, forgiveness, love, courage, tenacity, trust, discipline, and the ability to resist temptations and a host of other attributes and virtues. Only God has saved some marriages from disaster!

(When we see a couples together, we often marvel at their happiness but we must realize that there is a bridge over those deep troubled waters that has kept them together for so many years and a whole bunch of compromising.)

I currently wash my wife's tub out every morning and run her bathwater, open the door when she gets in the car and as we go into buildings. I often surprise her by cooking breakfast and dinner sometimes and giving her various gifts. This new me is older and wiser now, but I never did that stuff in the beginning of our marriage. I have changed her and she has actually changed me and we are both now two different people that are still married; but don't anyone think for one minute that it has been easy, quite the contrary, it has been tough and yet very worthwhile and rewarding.

I recall that on our first date, I purchased some wine, and as we were walking toward my apartment, she told me that she didn't like men that drink wine. Then she asked me, "What would you do if I busted this bottle of wine on the concrete sidewalk." I said, without hesitation, "Sistah, I would call a Taxi and have them give you a ride home." She laughed so loud that we both started laughing. I knew then that she was someone special.

I treat her like a Queen, and she, in turn, treats me like a King. We call each other, My Love. I personally do not like men that mistreat their women and think that men who beat women are actually weak men. I have been married 40 years and I have never laid a hand on my wife. Of course, we disagree, but we discuss issues, we do not resort to violence. I have never slapped or punched her, nor pulled a knife or gun out on her, and vice versa. None of my kids can ever testify that I saw daddy hitting mama or mama chasing him down the street with a knife.

I think some men are misogynistic deep down inside, subconsciously they hate women, because they constantly defend the abuse of women or blame them for the violence against them. I think some men truly do not even comprehend the meaning of love and it is really sad that many of them have mothers and sisters. These anachronistic cave men seek to justify, condone, and perpetuate violence against women. I am not talking about all men, but definitely weak men that resort to violence against a gender that should be respected and protected as Malcolm X once said.

I would like to share some conversations between my wife and

I. Here is an example of a discussion between my wife and I:

Yesterday, my wife asked me to mail 12 envelopes. I put all 12 in the postal drive through mailbox. Today she asked me, "Did you mail the envelopes? "I replied, "Of course." She then asked me if I bought the stamps for the envelopes and I said, "No, you never told me to buy stamps. You simply told me to mail them." I said," I thought they already had stamps on them and didn't even bother to look. "She said, "Who mails letters without looking to see if they have stamps? "I said, "Apparently, I do." Anyway, there are 12 envelopes floating right now in the United States postal abyss.

Another example of our interactions: I took my wife to get her car washed as well as mine today. Afterwards, we went out to a restaurant to eat lunch and while she was gone from the table, I told the waitress, "This lady and I were actually out on our first date and I sincerely hoped that I scored."

The waitress laughed, smiled, and when my wife came back, she told her, "Congratulations on your first date." My wife said, "First date, why we have been married 40 years! "and then we all started laughing.

Another time, I decided one year to give my wife a surprise Birthday Party. I did not tell Hudena Jr, my youngest son, because I thought he might inadvertently spill the beans. I asked Jamaal and Mercedes. our teenage son and daughter, to help me coordinate the event. We invited all Jackie's family, friends, neighbors, and employees.

In preparation for the event, Jacqueline saw me talking on the phone to someone in our bedroom as she came out of the shower and became upset because I was whispering. She told me that she would not tolerate infidelity in our marriage. I decided then and there to only do this surprise birthday once.

The day finally came for the surprise, I took her out to a

restaurant while all the guests surreptitiously went to our house. Once we got to the restaurant, I told her I forgot my money and wallet and I needed to go back to the house. As we parked the car in our driveway and got out of the car and walked toward the house, she said to me," I hear something in the house." I said. "You are hearing things because there is no one in the house", and then she said it again, "I hear something in the house." I replied, "That is just your imagination" and then I opened the door, and everyone shouted, "Surprise!" My wife took off running down the street in the dark of night. She thought someone had broken in the house. I have never seen her run so fast in my life. My nephew Anthony ran after her and said, "Aunty, it is a surprise birthday party." As I walked into the house, alone, everyone asked, "Where is she?" I said, "Running down the street." She finally came back, and we all laughed together. She told one of her friend, Lynetta, "I just talked to you a couple of days ago" and her friend said, "You do not know how hard it was not to tell you" and we all laughed again. It was one of the best moments of our lives. I also now realize that if a real burglar ever breaks in our house that I will not have any backup.

This is my philosophy on relationships Never get comfortable with your mate because someone is always on the bench that actually wants to get into the game and play ball with your mate.

In my mind, there are three stages of relationships: The first stage is <u>the innocent stage</u> filled with flowers, candy, gifts, numerous texts, phone calls, dinners and lunches...... you will simply call just to hear her breathe on the phone.

This is often followed by the second stage which is the <u>comfortable stage</u> of the relationship. In the comfortable stage, you two seem to take each other for granted. You simply do not compliment her looks any more. She buys a new dress, or hairstyle, and you do not even notice. He comes homes from work and the food is ice cold and amorous advances are meet with not tonight. An amorous mood now even competes with what is on the television set. A night out now is McDonald or Burger King. She undresses and you tell her to move out of the way because the Lakers are playing on television. The fire that raged is now actually cooling off.

You have to keep the fire raging in your relationship or otherwise the relationship will enter the third and final stage which is <u>the ICU stage (Intensive Care Unit!)</u>

This means the relationship is in a critical phase, you argue about the top not being on the toothpaste, the toilet seat being up is a full pledged argument. You spend more time with your boys than your lady, and you drive the long way to get home. At this stage, you two need counseling and communication and some more logs in the fireplace.

Do not ever take each other for granted. What you deem to be trash may be a vast treasure to someone else.

One day I went to my wife's classroom at Riverside City College. She was lecturing to about 50 or 60 college students and I walked in the room and from the back of the class yelled, "May, I add this class? "She, of course, responded, "No, it's too late to add." I said, "I do not want to add the class, I just want to see the teacher because I heard that she is fine." She started laughing and her entire class started laughing as well. As I left the class - smiling - I heard some of them say that is her husband!

Also, a lady at the law library recently asked me my name today and she told me hers. She said, and I quote, "I see you in here all the time with your daughter." I said, "That is not my daughter, she is my wife." She said, and I repeat, "Oh, she is beautiful."

I said, "Thank you." As we parted, I said to myself, "Damn, am I looking that old these days?" I told my wife and she actually think that it is funny!

Reflecting on the past, specifically the 1980's, I can remember going to pick my wife up from work one day and this guy approached her as I drove up to the sidewalk where she was standing. I jumped out of the car and yelled, "What do you want?". He mumbled and said, "I was going to ask her the time". I said, "Ask someone else the time or buy your ass a watch." He looked at me and simply walked away. I wish I could apologize to that guy. I was so insecure at the beginning of our relationship. Now, she gets hit on by students and I simply laugh; in fact, a man told her just the other day that she was very attractive and I simply smiled and said thanks; but back in the days, I was truly a mess and totally out of control. Thank God for age and maturity.

I believe the secret to marriage is true and genuine lovemaking is to be done both vertically and horizontally, but vertical love making should always precede horizontal. Put another way, mental persuasion for lower invasion. In the words of Shaq, can you dig it?

We now travel a lot these days. I love to take vacations. I have been to Bahamas, Mexico, Cabo San Lucas, Puerto Vallarta, Atlantis in Bahamas, St Thomas, Antigua, Hawaii, Park City, Utah, Santa Barbara, California, and Puerto Rico. I have also been to Disneyland and Disney World, Atlanta, Georgia and Montgomery, Alabama as well as; as Minneapolis, Minnesota. As soon as this Covid 19 is over, I want to visit Africa.

I also like driving a Mercedes Benz E350 these days and my wife has a companion Mercedes Benz 300. We have also given a Mercedes Benz C230 to my daughter Mercedes and sold one of our Mercedes to a dealership. I also like coaching basketball, football, golf, and track. I also collect stamps.

In the future, I would like to repair old homes and sell them. Flipping houses and then reselling them is my new goal. Also,

I want to buy real property in outside states and fix them up as well and resell them. Finally, my magnum opus will be to make a movie about an Egyptian woman being torn between her lover and her family.

# Chapter 3

# The Struggles

My wife and I struggled early in our marriage. We caught the bus to wash our clothes at various laundromats and even struggled to pay rent. I would hold a job for a few years and then abruptly quit to start my own business, in vain. In the interim, we had 3 kids between 1980 and 1987, Jamaal, Mercedes, Hudena Jr, and I had one son from a previous marriage named Paul that was born in 1976. I was proud of the fact that I had no unwed kids.

We struggled to feed and clothe them, and I can remember spending my last pennies on Pampers, diapers, and even writing bounced checks just to feed my family in those days. We would often time how long a check would take to get to the bank. For example, we would write a check at Gemco Department Store on a Friday and hope it wouldn't get to the bank until Monday or even Tuesday, thus giving us more time to come up with the money to cover the check. At one-point Sumitomo Bank threatened to close my account for so many bounced checks. I threatened to sue them if they did because I argued they had benefitted from my misbehavior with exorbitant fees from all my bounced check and that I would sue them for breach of implied covenant of good faith and fair dealings inherent in every contract in California. They backed off of the threat and I continued to write bounced checks.

I remember going over y to my wife's Aunt named Aunt Hazel. In the early part of our marriage, we went over her house and she offered us something to eat. We are being young and prideful said, "No", even though we were starving to death.

When we got ready to leave her house, she gave us a bag full of groceries. She knew we were starving, and our pride wouldn't let us admit it, but she simply knew. Thank you, Aunt Hazel, for reading our nonverbal signs bank in the days.

I have witnessed two bankruptcies in my life, one repossessed car, and unlawful and untimely evictions as well as subsequent lawsuits. I once had a Dodge Aries repossessed and yet because I knew the law, I was able to sue and get it back from the repossessers. I remember getting my car back and as I slowly drove off the lot in my Dodge Aries, I noticed Cadillacs, Buicks, Lincolns, and BMWs, still in the storage yard, but I was able to drive away based on my knowledge of the law. I also went to the Lakewood Sheriff Station that same day and picked up my gun that was in the repossessed car. Although, I did not pass the bar exam to become a lawyer, my knowledge of the law would be a noticeably big asset in my subsequent successes in life and that knowledge would rescue me time after time.

However, our lives really didn't change much, for the most part, until we moved away from Long Beach and bought our first house in Riverside, California in 1990. My dad had died in 1977 and my wife's brother, Robert, had bought a house in Fontana in the Inland Empire and encouraged us to move out his way. I hesitated because Long Beach was my home, but one day a guy that lived upstairs in our apartment complex came downstairs with a machine looking gun. I asked him why he was toting that powerful gun around the kids playing on the courtyard of the apartment complex. He said, I do it in order to protect the neighborhood." I decided it was now time to move. We sold everything in our apartment in a yard sale that weekend and raised enough money to move and put $10,000 down on a house in Riverside. My sister Ramona also loaned us $1000 and my brother Othello gave us $2,000 and my wife's mom gave us a $600 loan. We were almost 10 years into our marriage when we bought our first house in 1990. President Bush was President of the United States at that time and I wrote him a letter and told him I was having a hard time getting a home loan from the VA to buy my first house. I do not know what the President of the United States said or did, but the next thing I knew was that my loan to buy a $170,00 home in Riverside was approved by the V.A.

My second struggle was internal, I often struggled between right and wrong before buying that house. The Asians call it the Yin and Yang. Christians call it a battle between the flesh and the spirit. Muslims believe there is a contrast between Truth and Falsehood. Scientists allege that it is the conscious and subconscious in conflict, but regardless there is a battle taking place within each of us. The problem was that my dad liked to chase women and I found myself in that same mode chasing after women like a dog inexplicably chases after a cat. I could be with a woman and still chase after others. I battled this id and super ego for years and did not really mature until I bought a house. I finally realized one day that the best woman in my life was with me all the time and the outside temptations failed to compare to what I had all these years. I then turned around and started to appreciate the bird in the hand instead of the two in the bushes.

That maturity finally changed my life. The saying that character is destiny is true because as soon as I change my character, my destiny in life also changed. I acquired a house, nice cars, traveled, and begin to build a saving account. I realized chasing after what I already had was a waste of time, it reminded of a cat or dog chasing their tail. What is the point of chasing a car that I obviously cannot drive? I then became focused on achieving goals in life and I became remarkably successful at acquiring things in life. I also realized that I had wasted a lot of years. Years that I could never get back. I saw that scattered light was ineffective against a target, but a focused beam of light could cut through steel.

In the 1990's, I was working in the law as legal assistant for people like Attorney Best, Attorney Rogers, Attorney Johnson, Attorney James, The Compton City Attorney's Office. While, my wife Jacqueline, was working for Pioneers in Carson, California and her job would often take us on all expense paid trips. They often took us on trips to Santa Barbara, California, Honolulu, Hawaii, Park City, Utah, Coronado, California, Catalina Islands, California. They would often give us $1,000 spending cash as well. Then after 15 years of service, she was abruptly let go. She was devastated at the departure, but she sent out resume after resume and got repeated rejections. Then one day she received several jobs offers to teach on the college level and that is where we both are now teaching business law courses and paralegal studies to college educated students. We accidently fell into teaching, but we both acknowledge that this is our niche and where we both belong in life.

I am saying all of this not to brag, but to give encouragement to someone who is thinking about throwing in the towel. Keep hope alive because your turn is coming in life. Stay in line and please do not get out of it. Life is full of ups and downs. When one door closes then another door will definitely open for you.

# Chapter 4

## Our Kids

My oldest son Paul is from my first wife. There are couples that faithfully wait while their man is away in the Army, but not my first wife. She messed around as much as I did in those days. We often confessed our love to each other but cheated on each other as if it was our duty. We told each other that we loved each other, but we both practiced deceit before, during, and after the marriage. If there was were ever two people that did not belong together it was her and I. Despite being warned by my dad not to marry her, I went ahead and took the plunge. My dad was so angry that I married her that he did not even come to the wedding. It was as if he knew it was doomed to fail. It was over a couple of years later.

My ex-wife's mom really did not like me either. Her mother was well -to-do and they had considerable money. Her mother felt her daughter could do much better than me. I didn't heed either her mom or my dad's advice, but I definitely should have listened to them both. I tried to prevail against their opposition and prove them both wrong, but all I actually did, in life, was prove them both right.

One time, my car broke down over my first wife house, when

she was my girlfriend, and her mom refused to give me a ride home. I had to walk about 10 miles to finally get home. I walked from the El Dorado area of Long Beach to the Westside of Long Beach. Also, one time I broke up with my first wife, then only my girlfriend, and she took a knife and started stabbing a stuffed lion that I had won at a Carnival for her. My brother Othello said, "You shouldn't have broken up with her for merely stabbing a stuff lion." I told him that the stabbing of the lion was meant for practice on me and that I was next. Yet years later, I would still marry her. It is funny how love will make you forget serious issues under the guise of forgiveness. They say love is the equivalent of insanity because we actually lose our mind when we fall in love.

In spite of all this, we still married each other after I got out of the Army in 1975 and a year later had a son named Paul. The next year we were separated. We argued and fought almost every other month. My dad even came over the house one time and she busted all of our dishes right in front of him as we were arguing. I knew he was saying to himself deep down inside- I told your stupid ass that you shouldn't have married her- but he never humiliated me in front of her.

I realize now that it was the fact people didn't want me to have her in my life that made me want her so much. The wisest thing we both did in life was go our separate ways. The tragedy of the divorce was my son, Paul, was torn in his love for his parents and ultimately decided to give a preference to his mom's side and that may have brought dire consequences to his own life.

Years after we separated, I would later meet one of my first wife's Junior High School classmate in law school and subsequently marry her. My first wife would in typical fashion, that is her nature, tell everyone that I had married her best friend and tell my son, Paul, that I left her and him for her best friend. My first wife did not want to get back with me initially after we separated, but she would convince Paul that I left them both for my current wife and I would never ever be able to undo the damages caused by that lie.

My son, Paul, works with his hands these days, he does construction work, plumbing, and electrical work and has about 11 unwed kids. He has abandonment issues and does not have sex with protection. He alternates between anger and forgiveness and with me and right now he is in anger mode again. My wife and I have been in this new house for 4 years and he has not visited us once.

My current wife and I did go visit him in the hospital when his head were cracked opened with a golf club in 2019 by his enemy. But other than us making a serious effort to reach out to him, we rarely see him. I believe he will come around when he is ready. He is 44 years old now. Like I said before, his mom convinced him that I left her for another woman, but the truth is I begged his mom to come back to me after we split up, but she refused.

My ex-wife wanted to play the field as if she was missing out on something in her life and she was always looking for something better. She once told me we could get back together once her boyfriend from Kansas City left for Kansas. I said, "You want to have sex with another man from Kansas and then come back to me afterwards." She said, "You can't look at it that way." As I said before, we were not meant to be together.

I did not directly raise Paul, but I did visit him as often as I could visit him, and he would also visit me. The child support and child visitation would become contentious issues with his mom. She and I were often in court battling over those two issues. She wouldn't let me see him and I wouldn't pay support until she did. He got older and suddenly he didn't want to listen to me at all.

His mom had been raised around all girls and she didn't really know the first thing about raising a boy. She failed miserably at the job in my opinion. Once she couldn't handle him, around 16 years of age, she thrust him on me to change his behavior, but it was simply too late. He would come to stay with me at 16 and then leave my house abruptly. He said he didn't want to stay with me anymore and then subsequently moved back to Long Beach. Later that year, he drops out of high school at Long Beach Poly in the Eleventh grade and then begin a descent into the abyss of life. He got a woman pregnant in high school and would have baby after baby, never marrying most of the mothers. At last count, I think he had 11 unwed kids. He feels he is grown and that I can't tell him what to do.

One time that I recall was when Paul went to Knotts Berry Farm with his cousin Anthony and his brother Jamaal. When I came to pick them up at the spot where we arranged to meet that night, Anthony and Jamaal were there waiting as they had promised, but Paul wasn't. I had to go look for him. I chastised him for disobeying me and even yelled at him and then took him home to his mother's. The next morning, I went to get in my car and the front glass window of my car was busted. I suspected Paul did it.

Another time some gangbangerss did a drive by of a house on the Eastside of Long Beach. As they were speeding to get away, they ran a red light at 20$^{th}$ and Atlantic and hit the front of my car as they quickly drove by. I didn't know they had done a drive by, so I chased after them in my car. Block after block, turn after turn, and after about three minutes of these maneuverings, all four guys jumped out the car and ran away.

I saw Paul later that week and I said were you in that car? He said, "No." I said, "Why would 4 guys that had done a drive be scared of me?" He just laughed. The car that the gangbangers were driving was stolen a block from where Paul lived on the westside. I say to this day that they jumped out because he probably said that is my dad chasing us. It was as if God wanted me to see what was going on with my oldest son descending into the abyss of life and try to rescue him, but it was simply too late.

The good thing about my separation from his mom was my grades in college soared after I left her. My creative juices flowed like never before in my life. I started the Black Law Society at CSULB and become smarter and wiser President of the organization.

However, my ex-wife would often use my son as a pawn in a chess game to deny me visits and circumvent the will of the court. I would subsequently withhold child support because of non-visitations. I even got thrown in jail for not paying child support one time. I tried to explain to the judge that I withheld support payments because she would not let me see my son. The judge said, "Child support and child visitation are mutually exclusive and not dependent on each other." He further added that I should have still paid even if she denied visitation. The judge then threw me in jail. I argued that he could not throw people in jail because of my debts according to the U S Constitution which states debtor's prison are illegal. The judge said, "We are not throwing you in jail for your debts but for contempt of a Court Order to pay child support" and so I spent 30 days in jails.

My ex-wife just called me today and said my son Paul was messing with an M-80 Firecracker and blew off his fingers. The doctors were able to reattach all of his fingers except the middle one. A sad set of tragedies for my first-born son but I still love him even though he rarely calls me on Father's Day or my birthday. He reminds me of my father, however, in that he loves to fish in shallow and deep water just like my dad. However, my oldest son has mixed feelings toward his own dad.

I love you son and have always wanted the best for you in life. I sincerely wished that I had raised you from a baby because I know your life would be different.

My second son is Jamaal, I was coming out of the 99 Cents Store recently and he drove by. (Some of my friends are so rich that they may not even know where this store is located. I say that because many high-class people avoid low class stores. Anyway, it is the store where the rich take off their makeup and wear wigs to go inside the store to buy something. It is also the store where all the so-called middle-class, put on a veneer of poor clothing and shopping for the discounts.) I love the toiletries at the 99 Cent Stores more so than the food and I often stock up in volumes. Anyway, as I was coming out of the store and bending over to put my merchandise in the car. My second son, Jamaal, drove up and said, "Hey dad!!" I turned around and said, "What are you doing over here? "He responded that he was buying Chinese food for his wife and kids. Wow, at that moment, all I could think of was the Cat Stevens' song where he says, "My boy has grown up to be just like me! " It was a pleasant surprise and we talked about nothing, but in both of our eyes, you could see that we were happy to see each other and as he departed he said, "Dad, thanks for all the encouragement that you give me in life."

Wow!! My son is just like me!!

My son Jamaal was beat up in the shower by some of his fellow football players in High School. A girl in the church told me that she had a dream that Jamaal was attacked by vicious dogs. I confronted my son and he confessed that other football players had jumped him. I sued the school, the coach, and every player that jumped him. We finally settled out of court with most of the defendants.

My son Jamaal ran track in high school and college. I knew he was fast when we went to the beach one day and he ran against some older kids and beat all of them. I put him in football as a child and he ran track as a teenager. He ran the 400 meters in a best time of 46 seconds in a college race and won many races along the way. At that time, he was about 2 seconds off of the U.S. records and 3 seconds off the World record.

He won the high school championship in the 400 meters at Jurupa Valley High School and won a scholarship to Nicholls' State University Colonel track team in Thibodaux, Louisiana. He later transferred to my Alma Mater, Long Beach State University (CSULB) with another scholarship in track. Track literally paid for his college education.

My son Jamaal runs the same 400 that I also ran in high school but I could never run it under 50 seconds and yet he ran a 46 second 400 meter. His sister would later join him at Nicholls and ran the same 400 meters in 59 seconds. Jamaal would later graduate from CSULB to become a Los Angeles Police Department Officer (LAPD) in the tradition of his granddad, James Young, and his uncles, Robert Young, Kelvin Young and Sheriff Melvin Young.

Eventually my son, after 11 years, would resign from the LAPD and become a computer programmer, computer repairer, and truck driver. He would also file a stress claim against the LAPD. He also owns his own business that has him dressing up as a clown and promoting kids party and he has his own DJ Business that spins music. He also makes movies, hires actors and actress for his movies and draws and paints pictures. He is highly creative.

One day, my son went to rent a building in Riverside for an upcoming function. He called me to tell me that the manager of the building said," I know your father, he helped me with a legal matter many years ago" and so she gave him a substantial discount on renting the building. His phone call really warmed my heart. The good or bad that you do for others in life can often come back to bless or hurt your very own family. I love cyclical good.

Jamaal, you are a wonderful son. I love that you spend time with your kids. You are truly a great dad. I love how you love your wife Michelle. She is truly a great woman and you two make a great couple. I love that you graduated from college. You are a great computer programmer and businessman. I also love that you own your own home. You really make us proud. You own several businesses and you are overly ambitious and that speaks volumes.

My third child is my only daughter, Mercedes. I call her my favorite daughter because she is my only daughter. I cannot say enough about her. On March 31, 2017, I went to Arrowhead Regional Hospital in Colton, California because my only daughter was hit in the rear of her truck by a big rig truck. Her vehicle flipped over several times and then landed upside down with the roof of the car on the ground. Some good Samaritan saw her inverted in the vehicle and busted out her window and was able to get her out.

She was medically evacuated by helicopter to the nearest hospital. She has a lot of scraps and cuts but no spinal cord injury or disability. Thank God she is safe, and he protected her from severe injury. Thank God that she had dropped all her kids off at school and they were not in the car at the time of the accident.

Her brother, Jamaal, came to the hospital and was crying and my daughter was also crying. I am simply happy she is still alive and will be okay. I want her to bury me. I do not want to bury any of my kids. I love my daughter. She went out for her basketball team in the tenth grade of high school and was disappointed that they put her on the junior varsity team.

I told her to blossom where she was planted. She heeded my advice. The first game of the JV season, she made so many points in that game that the coach immediately promoted her to varsity. Never, Never, never let others limit your potentials in life! Shine like the Sun in life.

Another thing I remember about Mercedes was she disobeyed her mom and went to Las Vegas as a teenager. She came in the house innocently and her mom said the Spirit of God told me you went to Las Vegas and Mercedes was shocked as my wife read her the riot act. She never did that again.

Another thing I remember was Mercedes was 2 or 3 years old and she suddenly disappeared in a Gemco Department Store. Someone had obviously got her attention and we couldn't find her anywhere. I ran to the front of the store and told the guards to lock the doors because my baby girl was not in sight. The guard said we can't do that. I said my daughter is lost and I ran out and came back in through the exit door. The guard said you can't comeback through the exit door once you leave the store and I said. "Fuck you. I am looking for my daughter" and then out of nowhere she appeared. She said she was talking to a nice lady. I really made a scene that day, but I was genuinely happy to see her. Many people lose their kids and never see them again.

I still remember when I took my daughter, Mercedes, and my son, Hudena Jr to a Laker's basketball game. She was about 12 years old and her brother was about 7 years old. My daughter saw the singer and actor, Brandy, sitting in the stands and they were simply in awe. Although we were seating in different sections of the arena, I told her to go meet her, but security simply would not let her get pass to Brandy's area. I told her that if you really want something in life than you must find a way to get it and for her to go ask the security guard again to let her into Brandy's area. She and her 7-year-old brother both walked again to the same area and this time the security turned his back and they both immediately walked up and talked to Brandy.

My daughter and her brother were so elated and happy about the encounter. She said, and I quote, "Daddy, I actually talked to Brandy. I actually talked to her and received a hug." She felt good and that made me feel good because she was so happy. My daughter and son will never forget that encounter and just think, my daughter is all grown up now and an author of three books and one day Brandy may actually buy one of her books and my son is a helicopter pilot flying high in the sky and he may take her for a flight one day.

Mercedes, we love you. You never cease to pursue your dreams. You now have your BA degree and master's and are completing your doctorate - simply amazing. You are an author of three books and a wonderful mom and wife. You are sergeant first class in the Army, and you have been stationed in Kosovo, Italy and came back home safely. You love your husband, Alister, and he loves you. The two of you have achieved wonders together. You have a wonderful family and a beautiful home.

We were was so proud when you bought your lovely new home. You are a great daughter and very witty and funny and we love you. Keep pursuing your professional goals and stay up.

My last son is Hudena Jr. He meandered in life after graduating from high school. He went to Riverside City College (RCC) and did poorly in his college courses and when I confronted him about it, he said it was because it was a two-year college. He was doing poorly at the very school where I teach. He then transferred to CSSB, a four-year college, and repeated his same poor performance. I told him he had to leave the house because I would not subsidize his poor performance in school. He said, "Dad, what am I going to do, where will I live." I said, "I do not know. You may want to go into the Army, but it is your choice, but you can't stay here." He surprised me by joining the Army and being promoted as a sergeant within two years and then being sent to school to be a warrant officer and then to school to become a helicopter pilot. He has excelled in all his courses and we were all excited about his successes. The Army made him take life seriously and he simply blossomed. He is currently training to fly Cessna Airplanes.

Another thing I remember about Hudena Jr is that he wrecked my Black Lexus. He didn't call me, but instead called his brother Jamaal. All I heard was Jamaal saying late at night, "Whoa, Whoa, are you okay? I told my wife that night that I bet he wrecked my Black Lexus and finally he called me and said he had wrecked it. We went to visit the scene of the accident and parts were strewed all over the highway. It is simply amazing that he actually lived. Apparently, he was racing another youngster and his tire on the Black Lexus blew out. He hit a brick wall and then zigzag into a highway cement divider and then zigzag into a brick wall again and yet lived to tell about it. I was angry at the loss of the car but certainly glad that he was still alive.

The story that I like to tell people about my son, Hudena Jr, is that I always told him to water the lawn in front of our house every day after school and every day he did as he was told. However, one day it actually rained and as I drove home from work and I wondered if he would still obey me or use his common sense and not water the lawn that day.

When I came in the house, I said, "Did you water the lawn today?" and he said, "No daddy, I didn't water it today because it was raining."

I was happy to know my son actually had common sense because some people don't. Some people are so rigid in their thinking that they would have watered the lawn in the rain and swear they were being obedient to a command. Common sense is just not common, but it is indeed what separates us from robots.

Hudena Jr is a great golfer and we often play Golf. He has served and survived a year in the war zone of Iraq and is now an Officer in the Army and a leader of men. He is asking for his wife's hand in marriage this Saturday and I wish him and

Shavonne the best that life has to offer. You are your own man and you are making your own paths in life and in the world. Keep striving to succeed and I wish you and Shavonne, the women that you love, nothing but the best that life has to offer.... we love you!

Hudena Jr.....You are an amazing son. You ran cross country at a phenomenal pace in high school and I cannot thank you enough for all the basketball championships that you help me to win as your basketball coach. You simply refuse to fail in life and always got back up when you were knocked down in life. You amazed me by becoming a warrant officer in the Army and again by becoming a helicopter pilot. You are indeed focused and determined and I am proud to have you as my son. Stay ambitious and hungry and be all you can be in life.

Isn't it funny in life how serious stuff becomes quite funny as the years go by?

I remember our son; Jamaal and our daughter Mercedes were about 10 and 8 years old and my wife and I came back from shopping and we smelled the scent of cooked food in the house. We had told them to stay out of the kitchen, but they decided in our absence to try to cook pancakes and eggs. They adamantly denied they had done anything wrong. I checked the pots and pans and they were still wet from recently being washed. They had cleaned up well but failed to remove the scent from the air. They were caught! We laugh about it now that they are adults, but it was not funny back then.

I also remember, Hudena Jr, came in the house crying and said his brother Jamaal had hit him and I told him to hit him back. Those words gave him power and he went back outside and hit Jamaal real hard and said my daddy said I can hit you and he stopped crying and went back to playing. I laughed at his tears drying up so quickly and his confidence stirring up as he said my daddy said. My words had caused him to have bravado against his older brother.

Hudena Jr was taught how to play chess by me. What is ironic is that he was beating me in Chess in the 6th grade. We took him to Detroit and he beat his Uncle Elijah and then we took him to a Chess Club in Detroit and he lost the first game to the one of the best Chess Players there, but beat him in the second game. He was a beginner in Chess and the Chess Player in Detroit was a seasoned player. He got to the point where no one in the family could beat him. He also ran the 3 miles in cross country, and no one could beat him running at his high school.

Life is so coincidental, I went to Long Beach State University and graduated and my second oldest son, Jamaal, also went to Long Beach State on a track scholarship and graduated.

I was an E4 in the Army and my dad was a mere E3 and yet my youngest son, Hudena Jr, was a E6 and is now a warrant officer and my daughter, Mercedes, is a E7. They both outrank me, and I outranked my dad. They have both done drills at the same armory in Long Beach where I served. I was stationed in Ft Leonard Wood, Missouri for Army training as a Medic and my daughter, Mercedes took her basic training for the Army at the same place. Finally, what I find ironic is that I went to Long Beach Poly High School and so did my dad, Robert, and my oldest son, Paul.

I also remember the time we took the kids, Jamaal, Mercedes, Hudena Jr to Park City, Utah and played a pickup basketball game against four adult males and won. Another time we took the kids to Venice Bench and played a pickup game against 4 Adult males, Jamaal in the low post, Hudena Jr in the outside perimeter shooting threes, and Mercedes in the outside perimeter shooting twos and I was in the low post directing traffic. I thought we were the Harlem Globetrotters because we always won against our opponents. My wife Jackie, always cheering in the stands or on the court as our biggest cheerleader. We had some amazing victories as a family.

We finally took the kids to see my parents in Michigan and as we drove pass the place in Winslow, Arizona where the Meteor actually hit the Earth, the kids started screaming. The kids loved seeing the site. I had promised them that one day I would take them to see it and they finally saw the crater that the meteor had created. I also wrestled with my son Jamaal in the hotel and I kept shouting angry black man and laughing and joking with the other kids. When we finally arrived in Michigan, they saw snow for the first time. They loved the snow. They made snowballs and threw them at each other. My wife was shivering in the cold weather and Othello's wife, Sherri said to my wife, Jackie, "Girl, stop pretending, it ain't that cold' We all laughed.

One day I came home from work on a Friday and I told my wife, spontaneously, "Let's all get away and go somewhere. "We drove from Long Beach to San Diego and rented a motel and watched Madonna on television in a movie called Desperately Seeking Susan and laughed and laughed and laughed. We ordered Pizza and just enjoyed each other's company as laughter filled the room. It was a simple and sudden vacation that is an unforgettable moment in our lives.

# Chapter 5

## GRANDKIDS

My grandchild, Yasmin, who is 8 years old, was told by another culture at school today that she was "black." It was said in a very derogatory tone. The advice she was given by some in authority was to beat the girl up.

I disagree with that advice. My advice to her is that you are indeed" black" but she forgot to add the adjective - beautiful. You are beautiful and black and cherished and loved. When people try to attack our psyche, we must respond with positive reinforcement to quell foolishness. Turn what people intend to be lemons into lemonade by adding water and sugar to their negative remarks.

We are great in majesty and culture and no one should ever diminish our value or self-worth. God made no mistakes. Teach your children positive self-images of themselves and let them claim boldly that I am black and comely like Solomon and beautiful like the Queen of Sheba and I am a beautiful black stallion or mare. Give your kids a healthy sense of self. It will do wonders for them in the years to come as it did wonders for me. My teacher Mr. Brown in the 6$^{th}$ grade at Belle Haven Elementary gave me books to read that weren't given to the rest of the class. He taught me about famous Afro-Americans while I was in the 6th grade and I have given my kids and grandkids positive reinforcement of who they are in life.

Yesterday, I babysat my grandkids and took them to McDonald's to eat breakfast. One of my grandsons, Amare, the 2-year-old that only knows how to say "no", was eating pancakes with syrup when one of the pancake pieces fell on the floor. He immediately picked it up to eat it and my wife said, "No." She took it from him and threw it away. My grandson Amare responded by pushing the remainder of his plate away from himself in anger and refused to eat anymore and refused to drink his orange juice.

Then, unexpectedly, and suddenly, he abruptly jumped up and ran behind the McDonald's counter and into their kitchen as if to say to them- fix me another plate. I was surprised and so were the customers and employees as they grabbed him and returned him to me. I sat him back at the table and he still refused to eat his food. I treated him like my parents used to treat me and he finally got the message and started acting better.

However, his 5-year-old sister Yasmin told me that I was fired as a grandfather and that I wasn't her, Alonzo, Amare, or Alister Jr's grandfather anymore. I am going down to the unemployment office today to see if they pay fired grandfathers unemployment benefits. They were glad to see their dad when he came to pick them up and I was glad to see them go; but what is paradoxical is that I can't wait to see them again.

My other granddaughter is Anaya. She and her brother Jamaal Jr also known as JJ like to wrestle with me even though I always win, but they never give up. Both Anaya and Yasmin have won student of the month at their respective schools. JJ is a natural born basketball player and Anaya is highly creative and sells Girl Scout Cookies. The newest baby of the group is Mikayla, she loves talking on the phone with me and rocking in my granddad's rocking chair located in the living room of our home. My Uncle Dwight and his wife Yolanda gave me the rocking chair that Granddad Elijah used to rock in and Mikayla, two generations removed, loves rocking in it too.

I asked Jamaal Jr, what was the highest number in the world, and he said infinity and I asked him is there a number higher than infinity and he said infinity plus one. My other grandkid, Alonzo, wants to be a football player and I lost my voice watching him run a touchdown one day on the football field.

My son Hudena Jr doesn't have any kids yet and my grandson, Paul Jr., tried to write fraudulent checks on my bank account and steal money out of my bank account but I was able to get the money replaced. He tried to steal the money out of my Bank Account even after I had given him gifts of $750 and $1,000 to buy him a car. He threatened to burn down my house if I called the police on him and I went ahead and called them and had him arrested. Paul's other son, Trevon, has come over my house and planted flowers and pull weeds for us and gives me the utmost respect as does Cheyenne and Russell as well as his son King aka known as Chewy on the Internet. I have only met 5 of Paul's eleven kids.

I once had this exchange with 2 of my teenage age grandsons, Paul Jr., and Russell. They asked me yesterday, as we were in front of my house that is up for sale, "Did I know that a mass murderer lived across the street from me?" I acted in shock and responded with "No." They said, "Yeah, he killed his mother." I said, "What?"

They said, "You didn't know that he just got out of jail?"

I said, "No, what is his name?" They said, "His name is Wilson" I then looked at the real estate sign on my front yard and that was the "actual name" of my real estate agent. I tried to kill both of them. They were obviously playing a joke on me and got me hook, line, and sinker. They thought it was so funny.

I enjoy all my grandkids and wish them well in life and I hope those that are lost will return to the sheepfold.

# Chapter 6

## Robert My Dad

Today, July 30, is my dad's birthday. My dad was born on this day. He was born in a place called Elroy, Alabama. I visited Alabama in 2019 and saw Tuskegee Institute and the home of Dr. King but did not get the chance to go to Elrod.

My dad is no longer here but he made an indelible mark on my life. He would be 90 years old if he were still alive today. Enjoy your parents if they are still alive. You that have alive parents are indeed blessed. I sincerely thank God that my mom is still alive. She will be 86 this December 2020. My mom and my sister LaSharron share the same date of birth December 25, but in different years.

My dad was an amazing man and could fix any car problems and he owned a large collection of automotive repair books. He fixed cars for neighbors, family, and friends. They often preferred him over a regular mechanic. He once took a Cadillac engine out of a car and put it in a truck. He grew all kinds of exotic plants, raised, and sold fishes in aquariums, and repeatedly read books.

On Sundays, many preachers in Long Beach would gather at our house for alcoholic drinks and discussions about the Bible and religion and to tell jokes and talk about people in their churches.

His house was a type of Camp David where preachers could come and let their hair down. He left this Earth at the early age of 46 and yet he gave me so much courage and insights and strength. I remember him telling me that only a fool tries to please everyone and to always be myself.

After I got out of the Army at 21, I applied to CSULB and they rejected my college application. I told my dad that CSULB had rejected my application to attend their college. He told me to go talk to the Dean of Admissions and let him know that I was in the Army and that I had acquired a year and a half of college while going to school at night while serving in the Army. The Dean said a mistake had obviously been made and let me into the school.

When I flunked my written driver license test at 16 years old, he told me to get back in there and take it again and I passed. He would come to my track meets and screamed the loudest in the stands and if I was losing, I could actually hear his voice during the race, and it made me run faster.

When a bunch of boys chased me and my brother Othello home from elementary school, he made us get back out there and beat them all up or he said he would beat us up. My brother Othello and I went back out there and started swinging and all the boys ran home.

I miss you dad and I thank you for teaching me to memorize all the multiplication table in the 4th grade and teaching me all the Roman Numerals as well. I thank you also for teaching me not to fear any man and helping me to raise strong sons and a wise daughter. One day I will see you again, but until then - Salud!!

My dad once told me this story:

He said this Lion went through the jungle asking everyone who was the king of the jungle. The monkey, fearfully said "You are Mr. Lion" and the same question was posed to the Giraffe, seized with the same fear, said "You are Mr. Lion."

Finally, the Lion demanded to know from the Elephant who was the king of the jungle. To make a long story short, the elephant said nothing, but proceeded to whoop the Lion's butt. The Elephant took his trunk, wrapped it around the Lion and then threw him in the air. When the Lion fell back down, the Elephant kicked him into the trees, and then sat on him.

The Lion, still prideful, dusted himself off and told the Elephant, "You did not have to do all that stuff just because you do not know the answer to my question." It just goes to show that some people are so prideful that even in defeat they will not admit that they are wrong.

I remember when my dad and I went into the store with a bag full of soda bottles and it was after 7 pm. The man at the counter said, "I am sorry sir, we don't take bottles after 7pm." My dad said, "But I bought the sodas after 7 pm." The Clerk said, "That is just the store's policy." My dad said, "Well, who is going to clean up the mess." The Clerk said, "What mess?" My dad said, "I am going to drop all these bottles on the floor, and you will have to clean them up." He said, "Okay, turn them in."

Another memory I have was when I went to Mel Burns Ford in Long Beach to have my 1965 Mustang repaired as a sophomore in college. The mechanic said it was $400 dollars' worth of damages when I came to pick it up. My dad said they are ripping you off. My dad, knowing a lot about cars, told them what was wrong with the car and said I am not going to let you rip off my son. He asked the owner for the keys to the car and they said you cannot take the car unless you pay the $400. My dad said I have an extra key.

About a dozen white men stood in front of the entrance to

the garage to stop us from leaving with the car. My dad stepped on the gas full throttle and rushed toward them in the car like a bowling ball trying to strike pins and they all jumped out of the way. Once we got home, I was sure the police would be coming to the house to arrest us, but they never did come. I believe those mechanics knew my dad was right and that is why they never called the police. I, on the other hand, was young and naïve, but was so happy that I had a dad that knew about cars.

Another time, my dad gave a group of my young cousins that had gathered around him a one-dollar bill. To their amazement, he pulled out a "wad" of money at that time and proceeded to give to each of them a one-dollar bill. However, they upon seeing the wad, yelled for him to give all of them five dollars instead of "ones." He told them, "You all want five dollars?" and they cheerfully said," Yes, Uncle Robert."

He then asked each one of them for their one-dollar bill back and then walked away from them all and kept his money. They thought he was playing, but he was serious! He told them "the next time you get a dollar that you will appreciate it." My cousin Lydia told me that story about him and I still laugh about it today.

I talked to my Aunt Atherstine last night. She is my dad 's sister. She said my great granddad was named Obie Lee and his wife Virginia Lee traveled all over the country preaching the gospel and that he was a famous preacher back in the days. My grandmother, his daughter, Rozelle Lee, met her future husband, Elijah James, in Alabama at a church convention.

The two of them married and had ten kids. My dad, Robert, was the second of the ten along with his oldest sister Yancine, Ulato also affectionally known as Turk, Marvin, Obie, Reto, Alice, Geneva, Dwight, and Atherstine. Elijah and Rozelle would leave Elrod, Alabama and move to Long Beach to work in the Navy shipyards at the suggestion of Rozelle's brother, Fella Lee.

Fella took most of his family to Los Angeles while Rozelle's family settled in Long Beach. I once gave a family reunion with the help of Valerie, Jackie and Tommy Lavender that brought all the Lees and James together for a family reunion and years later Lydia brought us all together at a park in Lakewood and then Barbara brought us together for a reunion at a park in Long Beach.

Later, Elijah started the St Mark's Baptist Church in Long Beach. Elijah's father was Wesley James and his wife were Sophie. Sophie lived to be 104 years old. Elijah would preach at St Marks for years and then one day he and Rozelle divorced and he left and moved to Cheyenne, Wyoming and preached up there. My Uncle Dwight told me that when my granddad would walk down the streets of Cheyenne, Wyoming that even winos would get up from their drunken stupor and salute him with respect.

Another thing I recall in those days was that my dad, Robert, did not want me to marry my first wife and yet after I married her, he simply didn't want me to divorce her. He was fearful that if I left my first wife that I would be destroyed in life like he was when his first wife left him, but the opposite occurred with me. After he died in 1977 and I left her in 1978, I started to get A's in my classes and started the Black Law Society at CSULB and my creative juices started to flow, once I got out of that horrible marriage.

I don't think my dad realized that I also had some of my mom's genes in me as well. I did not go down after my divorce, instead I went up. As I begin to go up in life the attacks against me by ex-wife would increase. She would do anything and everything to destroy my current marriage, but all her attempts would prove to be futile. She even came over my house when I was not at home one time and told my current wife that she saw me with another woman. My current wife would destroy some of the living room furniture that day and then leave me. Her mother told her not to let that woman destroy your marriage and to go back home. A sincere thank you for my deceased mother in law- Queen Esther.

I also remember that my dad called everyone he met in life – "doctor." He only used it toward the male gender. I, however, tend to use it toward both genders, so do not be surprised or offended if I meet you one day and call you "doc" or "doctor." I am simply imitating my dad and maybe even the cartoon character Bugs Bunny, as well, and telling you that I think highly of you.

When my son Jamaal was five, he came into my bedroom one morning and told me that my dad, Robert, was knocking at the front door of my apartment and that he wanted me. Please understand that my dad had died in 1977 and my son was not born until 1980 and the year of this knock was around 1985. I asked my wife to go to the door to see what my son was talking about. She refused and replied, "He is your dad, so you should answer the door!"

I replied, "He will just be knocking on the door because I am not going to the door." To this day we do not know who was at that door.

One time, my dad whooped me with a fan belt in the garage for skipping school at Long Beach Poly High and I have been going to school ever since. He found out because the Vice Principal of Poly was his friend. I would decades later do the Taxes for the daughter of the Vice Principal that told on me. I still remember that whooping to this day. If you ever see me shaking, it is because I am thinking about that whooping.

My son Jamaal does not whoop his kids; he gives his kids a time-out. We did not know what time out was in our days. They gave us time up. However, some of those whippings actually saved some of our lives.

I remember my dad once told me that I could go to a party

at Silverado Park in Long Beach, but to be home by 11pm. Well, the fun did not actually start until after 11 pm in those days. My brother and I came home after 11 pm and my dad simply would not open the door. I thought he was playing, so I knocked on the door again. He never did open that door. My brother and I slept outside that night, but we never came home from Silverado Park late again!

I am thinking about, those days, and it is serious and yet also funny at the same time! Remember when our parents whooped us with a switch and then told us to go get the switch off the tree. Think about this people, isn't that like telling someone I am going to shoot you and I need you to go buy the gun? Let us not forget belts and extension cords. How did we ever survive those beatings? We would cry long after the whoopings were over?

My current wife would whoop our kids in a similar fashion, take a break, and then whoop them some more. I rarely if ever whooped our kids but occasionally I would. However, beating them reminds me too much of slavery.

My dad always said that a King only had a wheat crop one year and everyone that ate the wheat went crazy instantly. The King was perplexed because he knew the people had to eat something, but he did not want them to go crazy. He said to his assistants that I have some rice in storage, take a few people, and feed them that Rice and those eating Rice will always know the rest of us are crazy. He also said, 'Everyone in the world is crazy except me and you and I am starting to wonder about you."

Once when my first wife and I had an argument, she ran out of the house late at night and did not come back until the next day. I called her parents and they said she was not there, and I called my parents and she was not there. When she came home the next day, I asked her where she had been, and she said I spent the night at the Greyhound bus station, and I believed her.

The next day, I went to see my dad Robert and he said did you ever find your wife and I said yes, she spent the night at the Greyhound Bus Station. My dad said, and I repeat, "Am I raising fools?" He said, "The Greyhound station closes at 12 midnight." I didn't believe him and used his phone to call the Greyhound Bus Station and they confirmed what he had said was true. I would never forget those words...." Am I raising fools?" After our divorce, she would later tell my second wife that I will believe anything you tell him. Wow, I do not even want to think about all the lies.

Dear Dad, Robert James, and stepmom, Gloria James, you both are no longer here, but I just wanted to take a minute and tell you that O Shonda James (Mc Dowell) Onesimus' daughter received her Master's Degree the other day.

While I am at it, your daughter, Roberta James, has a daughter named, Marquita James, that has received her BA and her JD degree in law. Also, LaSharron's daughter, Lajuan has received her BA degree.

I hope you know, also, that your son, Hudena Sr, has a son, Jamaal, that has received his BA degree and a daughter Mercedes that has received her BA degree and her Masters and she is now working on her doctorate degree. Also, Hudena Jr is an Officer in the Army and flies' helicopters and small planes. I just wanted you to know that your grandkids are taking care of business. You may not be here to see it, but your grandkids are fired up and the fruit simply doesn't appear to fall far from the tree.

I am happy I had a dad and a stepdad in my life, they were both far from perfect and yet you could find virtues and faults in each of them. My Dad in Long Beach taught me to chase goals, religion, to pursue education, and strength, that is why sometimes I can be rigid and very resolute in my respective positions.

My stepdad in Pontiac, Michigan taught me an appreciation

of the arts, jazz music, and the inherent beauty of people and things in life. Both men, for better or worse, helped to shape and impacted my life and made me the Man that I am today.

"Do you love anyone this much?

My dad 's favorite poem was:
If I could give the trees a voice,
If to the rule of winds was my choice,
If I could make the ocean sing,
Sweetheart if I could do all of these things,
I would paint your name so true,
in the stars and sky up in the blue,
And if I go to heaven and you're not there,
I would set by the golden stair,
If you're not there by judgement day,
then surely, I would have known you went the other way,
and to prove my love is true,
I would come to hell to be with you.

My Dad loved poetry and fishing when he was alive. He would spend hours reciting poems and fishing. He loved fishing on the seashores, banks, rivers, and even went out on boats for deep sea fishing. One time a wave came and grabbed him off the rocks where he was fishing in San Pedro and took him out in the Pacific Ocean. He could not swim and always believed that it was a Miracle that he was pushed back to land by the waves.

I hate fishing and instead prefer to buy my fish at the store. I, therefore, thought that was the end fishing in our family line. However, my oldest son, Paul, has developed a love for fishing, just like his granddad, and he loves spending long hours fishing on the shore as well as going deep sea fishing on boats. My son loves it, despite the fact that he has never even met his Granddad.

Well, just now, my daughter called me and said my four-year-old Granddaughter Yasmin wants to go fishing and did I have any fishing poles. Is someone trying to tell me something? I finally took the grandkids fishing at the River next to my house and my grandson Alonzo caught a fish on his first outing.

Another thing I remember about my dad was one day, after I left my mom's house and went to live with my dad in Long Beach, he sent my brother and I outside to chop some wood. As I begin to chop the wood, I felt an asthma attack coming on. I ran in to the house to tell my dad, as was my custom to tell my mom whenever I had an attack. My mom would rush me to the hospital, and they would give me a placebo shot to cure the asthma. However, my father would do just the opposite, He shouted loudly in his bass voice in response to my urgent pleas, "If you do not get your ass back out there and chop that damn wood then I am going to whoop your ass." Those words cured my asthma immediately that day. It summarily went away. It was a miracle or either I was simply scared of my dad. One way or another, it was gone!

In the old days, not saying that I am old, you had to go down to the unemployment office building to apply for benefits if you were unemployed or needed a new job. The lines were always long and occasionally you would see two frustrated unemployed people in the line get in a fight.

One summer, after I was released from serving three years in the Army, I went down there and stood in the long line for about an hour and then finally saw a counselor about unemployment benefits.

We spoke formally for a few minutes and then informally for a few. Finally, she asked me who was my daddy. I said, "Robert James." She said loudly, "Robert James, is your dad?" She then repeated it again in disbelief.

That lady offered me all kinds of jobs once she found out Robert James was my dad. I do not know what my dad did to or for that lady, but she definitely rewarded me with a good job immediately. I told my dad and he just smiled but didn't give me any details. It simply confirms that a good name is better than silver and gold and that pays to know people.

The last thing my dad taught me was that belief is powerful:

Scientists say aerodynamically that the bumblebee is not supposed to fly.

Scientists are convinced that his or her body weight outweighs their wingspan, so therefore he or she shouldn't be able to leave the ground.

The only problem is that the bumble bee doesn't know this particular fact and so he or she flies anyway.

What if the bumble went to school and some esteemed professor told him what science said? The bumble bee may walk out of class and never fly again!

Your belief is powerful, and it can make you do what others think is impossible! Do not let anyone destroy your belief in who God made you to be in life. Do not let education, people, or anything else take away from who you are in life. You were born to soar.

My dad used to always say that most of us are just one missed paycheck away from homelessness. He also said that some people get quarter above their bus fare and all of sudden think they are better than you in life.

We should never really look down on anyone in this life. Just a couple of missed checks and the loss of our quarter (.25) and our economic class status and place in life would definitely change.

He taught me to treat everyone with respect.

# Chapter 7

## My Mom Josephine's Influences

My mom taught me how to read at 2 and 3 years old. My mom used to always say, "A hard head makes for a soft ass" and my dad used to always say, "A fool and his money are soon departed." She also taught me that life is full of distractions and interruptions. Stay focused on your goals. Rest if you must, but never quit in life were words from my mom.

She reminded me that an Eagle simply does not fly down and fight with a barking dog. The Eagle stays focused on flying and soaring in life. The dog barks at the Eagle because he or she wishes that they could fly like the Eagle. Her various lessons of life would stay with me to this day.

My mom was born in Kiblah, Arkansas. Her dad was Robert and he married Luesther and they had 4 kids, simply known as Jessie, Josephine, Robert aka Butchie and Jerry Wayne. My Uncle Jerry Wayne was always getting in trouble with the law and had several fights in high school. He finally settled down in his older age and died in a car crash a few years later. My Aunt Helen was very smart but made bad choices in life and one of her daughters, Sandra, was killed with a shotgun by gang banger over drugs. I attended her Sandra's funeral in Los Angeles, and they did not even open up her casket.

My Aunt Jessie liked to party, She and her husband Clarence aka Slim were party animals. They even partied with famous singing stars Ike and Tina Turner. My Uncle Slim was so smooth that he went to the actor Sammy Davis' funeral. He just walked in the service not knowing anyone and no one turned him away. They were a very sexy couple. One time my Aunt Jessie asked me to go get something out of her bedroom. I saw a book opened on her bed. I picked the book up and just started reading a few pages of the erotic book and the few words that I read gave me an erection. Apparently, she liked erotic books.

My Uncle Robert was a famous basketball player in high school, he should have been in the NBA, but he never made it because he got his girlfriend pregnant in high school, He worked for Fritos Lays for years and hooked me up with some good drug connections when I would later mess with drugs. He was very masculine and thus the name Butchie. He simply loved the ladies.

My maternal granddaddy, Robert, also loved the ladies and that may have led to an early divorce with my Grandmother Luesther. He came to my college graduation and once told my dad Robert, "Thanks son and I do not mean son in law" after a disagreement the two of them had. They had a contentious relationship because my dad would beat on my mom- his daughter -and he made no pretense about his feelings toward my dad.

My mom, Josephine, was unique and special, I once told her that she was not good at picking husbands and she just laughed. Her first husband beat her openly and her second husband beat her secretly. She claims no one understands her second husband and that he just has funny ways. Her second husband is very jealous of her and his insecurities often surfaces as he has accused her of flirting with other men when she is quite loyal to him.

My mom loved Sports, she yells at the Television like she is actually at the football, baseball, or basketball game. She was crazy about a show called the Fugitive with David Janssen about a doctor always running from city to city to avoid the police. The police wanted to arrest him for the alleged killing of his own wife.

My mom brought me a microscope when I said I wanted to be a doctor and took me down to receive an award for a poetry contest when I was at Pontiac Catholic High School. She would read to me as a baby still in the womb. Teaching me how to read was the greatest things my parents ever did for me. They taught me how to read and write before I even started school.

She was also instrumental in me getting my first job at Kroger's Grocery Store. My stepdad John once told me on the phone that your mom is so happy that you are teaching at college, but he never said that he was also happy.

This is a true story that occurred in Pontiac, Michigan when I was a mere 14 years old: My stepdad, John, would call me into their room and as they were both in the bed he would ask me a series of questions just to see if I knew the answer. My mom was obviously bragging on me as a scholarly young lad and he was so quick to prove her wrong. He would later tell me that it seems when people tell you that you cannot do things that you go out and prove them wrong. He tried to discourage me in my life's goals, but it did have the opposite effect. I turned all of his lemons into lemonade.

To my mom, Josephine, I thank you for giving birth to my life. I thank you also for walking me through a gauntlet of gangbangers that wanted to beat me up over a quarter (.25) at the skating rink in Pontiac. I still remember you walking me through them all at the skating rink and saying no one will lay a hand on my son. I was only 14 at the time, but I will never forget your courage and the respect the gangsters actually gave you. I love you mom!

The particulars of the skating rink fiasco are as follows: I was at the skating rink in Pontiac, Michigan, when a little boy dropped a quarter on the skating floor. The boy was about 9 or 10 years old. I immediately picked it up to give it back to him and this other teenager came out of nowhere and said it was his quarter and not the little boy. I gave the quarter to the older teenager. The little boy apparently had brothers in a gang called the Devils Disciples and he called them on the payphone and they came immediately to the skating rink and were all waiting outside the skating rink in two rows, a dozen on each side, in order to render street justice.

I thought they just might jump on me for giving the quarter to the wrong person. I called home and my mom came and walked me through that gauntlet of gangbangers lined up in two rows outside the skating rink and said no one is going to touch my son. I got in the car and looked out the window and the guy I gave the quarter to came out of the skating rink and those gangbangers beat him to a miserable pulp. He fought back in vain, but they soon overwhelmed him. Such is life in the ghetto.

Another moment I recalled in my life was when my dad Robert had died. I immediately called my mom and she replied," I am glad that son of a bitch is dead". "I said, "Mom. I am going to l have to let you go right now. I will talk to you later." As I grieved my dad's loss. I realize now that I had no one to talk to about his loss. He had alienated his former wife and his present wife with his fists. His wife Gloria would sell all of his stuff and moved to Louisiana after the birth of my sister, Rebecca. My mom definitely didn't like him and my stepdad John and my Uncle Slim said, "I was just like him." I grieved alone in anger for years and then one day God told me in a stern voice, " I am your Father and I can give you more than your Earthly Father ever could" and that is when I stopped grieving over his loss.

A salute goes out to all of my parents. I really owe you a debt of gratitude. My mom is still alive and will be 86 years old in 2020. She has gone from Baptist to Methodist to now Catholicism. She is a member of the Knights of Peter Claver Organization and aging gracefully. A couple times in my life I have drove over 2,000 miles from Riverside to Pontiac, Michigan to visit her with my wife and all our kids. I have also flown to see her, and she has flown out here. We went to a Laker game together and she was able to see Diana Lorena Taurasi, the WNBA star, play basketball in high school because we took her to my daughter's high school basketball game.

My grandmother made my mom the conservator of her estate and she made Jessie, her sister, the executor of her will. The two of them got into a conflict and Charles, Jessie's son, and I all of a sudden stop talking to each other because our parent were bickering about our grandma Luesther's estate and gift choices.

Prior to that dispute, my grandmother also found someone was stealing out of her bank account and she called me, and I contacted the bank when I realize someone was taking the very last check out of each of her stack of checks and cashing them. They had stolen close to $10,000 from her bank account. I was able to get all the money put back into her bank account after notifying the bank. The shock was that the culprits were one of her own kid and one of my uncles. My grandmother was so happy that she gave me $100 for my effort. She also said I knew I had put a hound dog on the case and that made me laugh.

My Uncle Slim once told my stepdad John that my real dad was not dead at my grandmother Luesther's funeral. He told my stepdad that I was the embodiment of my dad. His exact words were Robert is not dead, there he is right there. I don't know if he meant it as an insult or a compliment but he and I would never speak again as I accused him of being one of the culprits that stole money from my grandmother Luesther's bank account.

My mom and Jessie would also never speak again and at my Aunt Jessie's funeral the notable absence of my mom was blatant. My cousin Charles, my Aunt Jessie's son, and my favorite cousin, before we split, would die from drowning on vomited food while asleep on Thanksgiving night. I attended his funeral but was not allowed to speak. I still miss him to this day. It is so sad when families start fighting and it is often small stuff that causes big rifts.

My sister Ramona and my Aunt Jessie would become became really tight as the years went by and she was often torn between her love for her own mom and her love for her Aunt Jessie. I would never have such a conflict.

# Chapter 8

## JOHN AND GLORIA

In an odd coincidence, my parents divorced and both remarried people from the same city named Alexandria, Louisiana. John was my stepdad and Gloria was my stepmom. Little did I know that a city I had never visited would play such a crucial role in my life.

I almost visited the city of Alexandria when I rented a car and drove to Thibodaux, Louisiana to visit two of my kids, Jamaal and Mercedes, that were attending college at Nicholls State University, but I didn't because no one there would answer their phones.

Later that night, my car drove off the road into a ditch and I immediately woke up and drove along the ditch for a quarter of a mile and then drove back up out of the ditch and got on the road. My wife was in the back seat screaming we are going to die. Once I got back on the road, I told her everything is under control, but we never made it to Alexandria. My stepmom. Gloria would not return my phone calls and suddenly disappeared when I said I was near her home in Alexandria.

The good thing about having two moms in my life was that my mom and stepmom taught me the art of kindness and eating good foods. Both women helped to shape my life and taught me that kindness can go a long way. They were both very kind to me back in the days and made me the Man that I am today because of their various ways.

My stepdad, John, favorite saying was "Apply the stimulus and get the response" He said it so much that it became etched in my mind. He and I feigned like we liked each other to appease my mom. We never really got along. John wanted to control how I spent my money from my Kroger job and also started opening up my private mail. He would engage me in long talks at night until the early morning about a girl that wrote him a dear john letter for years.

My stepmother was Gloria. She was a great cook of Tacos and Catfish and truly kind to me while my dad was alive. She would often call me when my dad was alive and once even visited me in Fort Leonard Wood, Missouri to tell me that she had finally left my dad and was never going back. Then a couple of weeks later she would be seduced by his charm and return back to him in Long Beach and the recycling of mistreatment would begin again.

My brother Othello shocked me because he stood up to my dad and my stepdad when they hit our respective mom and step-mom. He physically fought my stepdad for mistreating my mom.

He almost physically intervened in my dad mistreating my stepmom, Gloria, as well. While my dad was beating on my step-mother, my brother Othello told my dad not to hit her anymore. I looked at him like he had lost his mind. My dad looked at him sternly and then told him in a loud voice to sit his ass down and he then came to his senses and sat down. Later, that day, my dad hit him in the chest for standing up to him.

I, on the other hand, felt Gloria should leave the house if she did not like the treatment, she was receiving from him. In short, run away, because that is what I was planning on doing. I was constantly planning my escape. She would leave him several times, but he was always able to charm her into coming back to him for more abuse. However, she stayed with him and endured the constant abuse with love and affection toward him and once he died, she received all his inheritance to the exclusion of his initial 5 kids. After my dad died, Onesimus told me that my dad left a holographic will, but the alleged holographic will that he saw suddenly came up missing and Gloria denied its existence.

I believed my brother Onesimus claims that my dad had an holographic will but it was never found and it would never surface and was repeatedly denied to be in existence by my step-mom Gloria and consequently any assets held by my dad were bequeathed to my step mom and her children to the exclusion of his initial 5 kids .

This exclusion of the initial 5 from his inheritance would anger me for many years until my Uncle Obie, Robert's brother, told me she deserved all of my dad's stuff because of the mistreatment and beatings that she had endured over the years. Although, I felt she had circumvented the will of my dad because I knew that he loved us too much to leave us nothing. I simply refused to believe he would leave us without any of his assets and so I was really conflicted over this matter.

My brother Othello said leave the issue of the Holographic Will alone and so did my sister Ramona. They did not want anything from our Dad because of how he had treated our mom, but I did not leave it alone. I threatened to sue Gloria and when she found out I was going to sue her, she threatened to file Bankruptcy. Then one day in a dream God said to me I am your father and I will give you more than your Earthly father ever could give you. I then forgave Gloria, invited her over my house for dinner in Riverside, California and when she came from Louisiana to visit and we made our peace.

Although, she and I made our peace, Onesimus, her son and

my half-brother, would become secret enemies. He jumped on me when Gloria came over my house to visit and eat dinner. He started wrestling with me under the kitchen table for the second time in our lives. The first time he jumped on me was over my sister Zoe's house in Compton. Onesimus would often jump on me and wrestle me to the ground when he had on tennis shoes and I was in a suit and dress shoes. Ramona pulled him off of me the last time and she shouted, " Get off my brother" and Onesimus replied, "But I am your brother too" and Ramona just looked at him and said nothing; while La Sharron's husband left the house when we were wrestling and went out to the front of the house.

Nemi's words often said he loved me, but his actions always showed that he despised me. Secrets that I told only him, he would go back and tell my ex-wife and even demean me to my brother Othello. He once told Othello that I was crazy for shooting a rat with a 22-caliber gun. Othello quickly told me to watch my back. Like I said, Nemi didn't like me and his actions often betrayed his kind words to me, but I liked him very much and would in vain take him to lunch and dinner and try my best to at least be friends.

I say he was ambivalent in his feeling toward me because he did ask me to be the best man at this wedding to Renee. He obviously liked me and yet disliked me at the same time. His dislike may have been because of the accusation I made about his mom, my stepmom, Gloria, not being able to find a holographic will from my dad that he swore he saw. I honestly don't know the particulars, but I do know his actions betrayed his words.

For example, one day, Nemi called me to tell me that he heard my son Paul had dropped out of school in the 11th grade. He said on the phone, "Wow, you are so smart, and your son did not even finish high school." I said, "What is that supposed to mean?" He said, "I was just saying!" But in reality, he was making a dig at me for accomplishing so much in life and yet my son quitting his educational journey so early in life. Years later, I would find out ironically that Nemi, himself, had also dropped out of school.

My encounters with my stepdad John were numerous, one time he asked me whether I had swept the kitchen corners. I said, "Yes.: and he replied, "Did you see the quarters in the corners?" I said, "No" He knew that I had not swept the floor because I did not find the quarters in the corners. He said it was an old Navy trick.

As a youth, John sent me to the store to buy him a bottle of 7 up. He would tell us we could not drink his 7 up in the refrigerator and that we were supposed to drink Kool Aid only. I would often drink his Seven Up and then put water in the bottle to replace the soda I had consumed. One time he sent me to the store to buy him a 7UP and I came back with the soda but told him I had been robbed of his change on my way back home. He ran out of the house looking for the thief, but the thief was me and I was in the house. I had spent the change on my favorite candy bar - a Butternut! That was me in those days.

He also told me that if I steal a car that I should steal a Rolls Royse rather than a Volkswagen because you get the same amount of time in jail. He would also pretend to whoop me when the doors were closed so the other kids in the house would think I was getting a beating when in reality he would just talk to me and hit the bed with the belt and tell me to yell.

My stepmother Gloria and my Uncle Dwight became a coterie of friends after the death of my dad. Gloria referred legal matters regarding my dad to my Uncle Dwight after his death. Gloria also started acting differently toward me after my dad's death. Talk went around the family that my dad had loaned some unknown person $2000 dollars just before his death. Whoever he loaned the $2000 dollars too never spoke up at the funeral nor never paid back the loan. I often wondered if my stepmom thought it was me because she never gave the initial 5 kids anything from his financial estate. She sold their house on Caspian St in Long Beach, his cars and truck, emptied their bank account, bought a station wagon and left California with my 4 other siblings from her and my dad in a hurry.

I would only see her twice after she left. Once she came back to visit her family and I invited over to my new house in Riverside for dinner because I wanted her to see that God had indeed blessed me in spite of being excluded from the holographic will issues with a two story five bedroom house and the second time was at my Uncle Obie's funeral.

The third time she came out to California was to bury her son, Onesimus, who suddenly left his wife and 4 kids to go live with a Mexican girl. When the Mexican girl wanted to leave him sometime later, he tied her up to the bed for threatening to depart from him after all he had given up for her. I guess he felt he had left his wife and 4 kids for her and now she was leaving him. He tied her to the bed and repeatedly raped her.

She finally asked him could she go next door to get some flour or sugar to cook a meal for him. When she went next door, she called the police. When Onesimus heard the police coming. He killed her young daughter by another man and then the daughter they had together and then took the gun and killed himself.

The ABC news channel asked me for an interview, and I explained that the family was shocked and devastated about Onesimus aka Nemi's actions of triple murder and rape. Some in the family blamed the girl but I blamed my brother for his actions. However, I never attended his funeral and afterwards my son Paul told me it was wrong for me not to attend my brother's funeral. I told him, "If you ever kill your kids that I will not be attending yours either" and he shut up. All my other brothers and sisters attended his funeral, but I did not.

After Nemi did all of those dreadful things, my sister in law, Nancy, came over our house to visit. I asked her if she had heard what happened with my brother Onesimus. Nancy said," I wasn't going to say anything, but sister, do you feel safe?" We all had a good laugh because she knows that I would never hurt my wife. Nemi and I may be brothers, but we were as different as day and night. My mom and stepdad didn't go to Onesimus funeral either. My mom told my family in Michigan and they were in shock. My brother from Detroit, who barely knew Nemi came out to California to preach his funeral. I was trying to find the mom to tell her how sorry we were for her plight, but she would never answer the door.

I started listing to a lot of Jazz in those days like Stanley Turrentine after my brother Onesimus' death. I wondered why he had not called me in his moment of stress. I then begin to realize that I had a love/hate relationship with Nemi and both of my dad's, Robert, and John. John did have some positive influence on my life. He taught me an appreciation for Jazz and appreciation for music. My real dad did not like any non-gospel music playing in the house. I think it was because it reminded him of my mom, but I do not know the real reasons for his nonplaying of secular music. My dad taught me the value of an education and promoted it throughout my life.

Many of the preachers in Long Beach would often pack our house and have drinks after church on Sundays. They would laugh and crack each other up about mess in the church. They talked about women, sex, and everything else. Little did I know at the time that one of those men, sitting in the living room of my house, would license me one day to preach the gospel. Nor did I realize one of the men in the house known as Red would be the Uncle of the woman that would later become my second wife. We truly live in a small world.

# Chapter 9

## Sisters and Brothers and Cousins

It was tough being the oldest brother in my family. I had to constantly stick up for my younger siblings.

My sisters and brothers are Ramona, Othello, Zoe, and Elijah by Robert and Josephine, then there is Ronald by Josephine and John and last but not least, Onesimus also known as Nemi, La Sharron, Roberta and Rebecca by Robert and Gloria. Rebecca has the distinction of being born after my dad died. She and Elijah would never have the opportunity to really spend time with our dad, Robert.

My sisters, Ramona, and Zoe were really close as kids but now they do not speak to each other at all and Elijah and I rarely talk these days. We each want our own way in this life, and we are becoming more stubborn as we age. We clash like roosters in a hen house these days. Our moms and dads had all Chiefs and there are no Indians (Native Americans) in the family or all Roosters and no Hens.

What is ironic is that Ramona, Othello, and I have had falling outs, but we always seem to make up and have remained close as brother and sister throughout the years. I simply cannot say the same for the rest of the family. Ramona and I fought like cats and dogs when we were little kids and now, we are very tight as adults. She wanted to see Shirley Temple as a kid, and I wanted to see Tarzan on television. Since they came on at the same time, my mom often gave preference to Ramona's choice over mine. I did not realize at the time that I was victim of gender discrimination and although my mom denies it, she certainly had her favorites.

I remember that Ramona was at my college graduation from CSULB in 1978 with my grandad Robert and my Uncles Dwight and Obie. I don't remember what the commencement speaker said that day, but I will never forget what Ramona said, her words remain with me to this day, "You said it and you did it." She has always supported me, encouraged me, and inspired me throughout my life. She is the oldest sister of my five sister and knows how to fight like a guy. She once beat up a guy that tried to snatch her purse. I think he retired from purse snatching after that incident. He came by on a bike and attempted to snatch her purse and she fought him like a man until he gave up the effort.

However, she cried like a baby when we moved from sunny California to the frigid winters of Michigan at the young age of 13. I love you sister, and this shout out is to you. An incredibly special shout out to the one and only Ramona - my oldest sister. She is currently a retired nurse and is often in the hospital, fighting hard to stay alive right now, while giving orders to her nurses and doctors. She raised one son and spent her life giving him all the luxuries of life only to have him grow up and turn his back on her.

My sister Zoe just called me recently. I did not recognize the number and at first and I was not going to answer the call. I have not heard from her in almost 10 years and so I reluctantly answered the phone call. We talked for about 27 minutes about everything.

Sometimes family members fight over the slightest things then as the years go by those things seem so very petty and insignificant. Apologies abounded throughout the conversation and the discussion was rich and very deep. We fell out because she told the family I didn't have any decent towels in my new big house and tried to order me around in my own kitchen at one time. Those of you that have family issues with one or two members of your family, stay really hopeful, maybe they will change one day or you will one day change, but remember that change is often good even in the dynamics of family. Zoe is extremely smart and often looks over my lawsuits for errors these days. She has a keen eyesight for typing errors.

My sisters Ramona and Zoe 's are not married. Ramona is now 65 and she still claims one day she is going to get married. Zoe is 63 and I do not see it on the horizon for her either. The recent marriage proposal to the 67-year-old model Beverly Johnson may give them some hope, but. I don't see it because my sister Ramona and Zoe are both too bossy and have too much masculine energy to work in tandem with any man. In short, they have never been married because they are too bossy. Also, their relationship with my dad and my stepdad were very unhealthy. Ramona claims my dad put his finger in her vagina and my stepdad pulled out his penis and said your mom loves this penis. Zoe also fought John with a belt and hit him in the eye and has had a bad relationship with my real dad, John, and me.

I remember Ramona went to a Drive-In movie with her date. She asked the date to buy her a soda. The date came back with a large coke and two straws. I thought that was very romantic. Ramona cussed him out for not bringing her a separate soda. She asked me was she right. I told her that I would have left her at the Drive-In Theater.

My brother, Elijah, did not see dad until he was dead. We

took him to view the body at the funeral home in Long Beach and he saw our deceased Dad and started crying. I had repeatedly asked him to come visit him when he was alive, but he never would. He saw John as his real dad and not Robert. He and I would later fall out over a measly $50. He is a Pastor of a church in Detroit. His first church was taken from him by deacons and trustees that locked him out of the church. He started his own church and made it a point to be listed as pastor for life in his bylaws. He had a really beautiful wife with a lovely spirit suddenly dies of cancer one day.

One day he mailed $50 to a woman in his church, while his wife was alive. He put my address on the envelope as the return address. The $50 in the envelope was undeliverable to the woman and so it came to me. He claims I never paid him back the $50 and I claim that I did, and he simply wants another $50 and we currently do not talk. He cuts me out of all his family pictures on FB, I have totally blocked him on my FB page.

He also said I was darker than anyone in the family, which is true, and I didn't work on cars like the rest of the family, which is true, and I didn't have a letter from my dad saying dear son, which is also true. He said I was not really a member of the family and thus not his brother. I am actually closer to my cousins than I am to my own brother, Elijah.

At first it bothered me, but as the years go by, we have slowly drifted apart in life. When he comes to Los Angeles and visit family, he makes it a point not to put me on his itinerary and when I asked him why, he just laughs. The last time I visited Pontiac, Michigan in 2019, I saw everyone but him. I simply believe we should taste our own medicine.

Although he claims I am not his brother, my mom has said I acted more like my dad than any of the kids. Thus, Elijah and I have had a serious misunderstanding of each other ever since that

$50 moment and it continues to get worse to this day. I simply do not think it is about the $50 anymore. I recently sent all my brothers and sister $40 a piece but I did not send him a penny.

He once told my brother Ronald that I abandoned him when I moved away to go to California to live with my dad in Long Beach. I was 16 and he was only 11 years old at the time when I left but I simply wanted to see my dad and I am glad that I did.

My sisters LaSharron, Roberta and Rebecca currently live in Alexandria, Louisiana. La Sharron is also a Pastor with her own church. Roberta is active in the church as well as stays in contact with me the most. She is the one that told me Gloria, my stepmom, was deceased in Alexandria, Louisiana. I sent flowers to her funeral. Roberta is a travel agent and I often purchase my airline ticket and cruises through her since the cost of living is cheaper in Louisiana. Roberta loved my dad and she often puts me in check when I criticize him or my stepmom. I understand her love for them both, but no one is above criticism and we all have virtues and vices. They come to Los Angeles quite often and always put me on their itinerary. We mostly talk by phone or texts these days. I remember one time when La Sharron first visited my wife and me. She saw our two-story home in Riverside and she spontaneously said, "You all are some uppity niggers." I could not believe she said it, but she did.

My last sister in Louisiana is Rebecca. She was born after my dad died and she does not really know me and there is no real emotional connection there besides the fact that we know we are brother and sister. I think if they had of stayed in Long Beach after his death that we would have been closer, but they left after my dad's death. They all moved to Louisiana, so we really do not have an emotional connection because we did not get to spend any time together, but she is still my sister although we rarely if ever talk.

My brother, Ronald works at the plant in Michigan as a supervisor and owned quite a bit of real estate at one time. I protected him as a little kid because my brother and sister wanted to use him as a scapegoat for the mistreatment they received from his dad- our stepdad- and I would never allow them to beat him up. Every time I visit Pontiac, he takes me out for lunch or dinner. He loves rap music and was married once and has never married again.

My sister Zoe surprised me recently and called our sister Ramona to wish her well in the hospital today. I cannot believe it. I have repeatedly asked her to call Ramona and finally she did. There is indeed hope for the Palestinians and Israelites if these two can come together. I thought it was mature on Zoe's part to call Ramona.

My favorite cousin on the maternal side of my family was Charles Lakey. He was like a brother to me. We partied in Los Angeles and Laguna Niguel. We attended the same CSULB college. Both of us went into preaching early in our lives and we both chased skirts and went fishing and then one day he died on Thanksgiving night and prior to that our closeness ended over a dispute involving our respective mothers and our grandma's will.

My favorite cousin on my dad's side was Robbie, he and I were tight until I joined the Army and then went to college. Our lives started going in different directions. He wanted things out of like that I no longer wanted, and we quietly parted company from each other. We still run into each other at funerals and family get togethers, but the emotional distant is blatant. He once told my wife Jacqueline that I said for her to write him a check. My wife said I do not even have to ask him because I know he did not say that to you. She knows me well and that is why I love her.

# Chapter 10

## OTHELLO

Othello is my favorite brother. My memory of him was that he had very quick hands and could box well. In fights, he would often hit you in a flash and then exclaim, "Did you see it?" Most people did not see the punches coming because they came so quickly, but they often felt the harsh sting of his punches before they could react. He was simply fast. In the words of Ali, he could turn off the lights in the bedroom and be in the bed before the room got dark.

He looked like a little bit like Muhammad Ali and carried himself with immense confidence as if he knew something about life that others did not know. My one regret in life was not taking him to a boxing gym when he was younger and having him train to be a boxer in life. He would have been a great one.

Growing up he feared no man and when we got on public buses, he would often kick people's legs out of the way in the aisles as he waked to his seat. He was actually challenging them to fight him, they never responded to his challenges. I remember when he was in the Air Force and he left his money on his bed and went and took a shower. He came back and his money was gone and so he beat up his roommate. His explanation was that the roommate took it or knew who took it.

He once stole a police car from the police and when I asked him why he had done it, he replied, "Wait until you steal one". I said. "I am never stealing a police car." He obviously sees the world differently than most people.

As an adult, he told his neighbor not to feed his dogs and his neighbor fed his dog anyway, so Othello took his neighbor's keys and threw them down the street drain. The police came to his house in Pontiac to arrest him and he told them to talk to his attorney on the phone. The supposed attorney on the phone was none other than me impersonating one. I talked to the police from California and told the Police in Pontiac, Michigan that I was his attorney and that they didn't have a warrant or probable cause to be in his house and they actually left. We often laugh about that to this day. I was not an attorney, but I have the gift of Gab and knew enough law to get them out of his house.

Many of the things Othello did surprised me, He was the first member of the family to marry. He married early in his life and was the first to divorce rather quickly. When his ex-wife asked for alimony,-he sent her some sunflower seeds and told her to grow them in response to her alimony request.

When he was younger, I could beat him up and we once fought all over the house because he would not take a whooping from my mother in Pontiac. Years later, I would not be able to beat him because his fists were simply too quick. We still often wrestle for fun when we met each other at the Los Angeles Airport or at the Detroit Airport, but we never actually fought each other again after high school.

I remember when all four of us brothers meet in Kansas City, Kansas to hear my brother Elijah preach at my great Uncle Oscar's church. Oscar was my grandmother Luesther's brother. Othello and I started wrestling all over the hotel room. He was about

300 pounds and I was about 180 pounds. Of course, I lost the wrestling match. Afterwards, my brother Ronald said "Hudena, I can't believe you actually stand up to big ass Othello and wrestle him like you do." I told him," I am the oldest brother and he has to recognize that fact." Othello responded, "Hudena aint no punk." He has always given me the highest praise and respect. The respect that I would never get from my brothers Elijah or Onesimus aka Nemi.

My Uncle Obie, the brother of my dad Robert, once told me that when Othello was attending college at the University of Wyoming that he walked into a party full of Black people and cut off the music and canceled the party and told everyone to go home. He was at that time a Muslim adherent of Elijah Muhammad and told all the party participants that Elijah Muhammad said, "We as Black People partied too much, and we needed to go home!"

I was told all the participants left and no one challenged him. My Uncle Obie stands by the story, but Othello denies that it ever happened.

We were so close that I even let him sleep with my girlfriend at Long Beach Poly High school. He had acne on his face and there was a rumor in high school that sex heals acne. Othello would later tell me that my ex-wife asked him to bed and he refused. He also once slept with a lady friend of mine as was subsequently revealed to me by Ronald. Ronald would tell me that Othello is sleeping with your lady friend. Surprisingly, I was angry at the lady friend and not my brother.

At Long Beach Poly, my brother Othello and Larry were on the same football team and one day they had a physical fight right in front of the school over something that happened on the football practice field. My brother, Othello, and he circled each other throwing punches. Othello's punches were quicker and landed more often. He would tease Larry while hitting him by saying,

"Did you see that" with a smirk. Each punch landed with precision to its target.

The fight was so one sided that my teammate on the track team, Elvie said, "I am going to jump in," and I responded immediately, "If you jump in then I will jump in too," and the fight remained fair between the two of them because Elvie didn't jump in the fight. Elvie and I practiced together on the track team and were close teammates, but he and Larry were the best of friends, but Othello was my brother and an attack on him was an attack on me. Later in life, a guy would jump on my son, Jamaal, and my daughter Mercedes immediately jumped in when the opponent's brother came to his aid. I guess you can say defense of family from strangers is genetically engineered in my family.

I recently posted a picture of my brother Othello on FB and Larry posted a response that said, said, "Does he remember that beating I gave him at Poly High" and I just laughed. He feels he won the fight and I feel my brother won it, but I guess it depends on who you talk to about the fight. All I know is that my brother Othello had the quickest hands I had ever seen in my life.

Othello and I were very mischievous as kids and we once went to downtown Pontiac, Michigan and stole all gifts that we gave to the family that year for Christmas. We were obviously young and rebellious. What is ironic is the one person I can't stand these days is a thief.

On another occasion, a guy ran to his car's truck after Othello made him angry at the Teen Center on Willow on the Westside of Long Beach. I presume to get a gun to shoot my brother. I said you are about to shoot Monte's cousin. My cousin Monte had an infamous reputation, and just the mention of his name made the guy immediately closed his trunk and drive off. Othello always had my back and I always had his back.

We are still tight and talk on the phone about 4 or 5 times a week these days. He gambles a lot in Detroit, Michigan and has won and lost a lot of money. He is considered a heavy Roller and has VIP status at the Casinos. Everyone knows his name and they call him Big O when he took me to the Casino to watch him play. He plays Blackjack extremely well and has won $30,000 at one time but he has probably loss even more. He gambles with the same passion that I bring to Golf. He won so much money one year that he bought the old house that we used to live in as kids from my mother and stepdad in Pontiac.

As he ages, he is not as aggressive as he once was in his younger days and is now more even tempered and has mellowed out in these latter years. He told me at the Casino that this guy owed him some money and I said, "Aren't you going to make him pay you" and he said, "No let him have it." I realized then that he had mellowed out over the years. He went into the Air conditioning and refrigeration business as a career and worked on the manufacturing of cars for Pontiac Motors. He is actually one of a kind and when we went to Detroit, I took him to play golf and to my amazement, he actually hit the ball over the Lake. Hitting the ball over the Lake is not an easy task for a first time Golfer but he did it with ease.

He claims he can beat me in a game of Pool. I have bought a pool table for our house and we will play one day as soon as this Covid 19 pandemic is over. He calls me and asks me am I practicing. This is probably going to be the one area that he cannot beat me in life.

# Chapter 11

## UNCLE DWIGHT

Dwight was the brother of Robert, my dad. My dad had two other brothers, Marvin, a preacher and barber, and Obie a probation officer. Obie went to the University of Wyoming and he tried to get me to go there after high school but instead I joined the Army. Marvin cut my hair and gave me advice as I sat in his chair. He also had a Black Belt in Karate.

My dad also had 6 sisters, Yancine, Ulato aka as Turk, Alice, Reto, along with great singers like Atherstine and Geneva. Alice and Turk were genuinely nice to me and always greeted me with a smile. Reto would listen to me as I went over her house to unload and complain about all the things that were going wrong in my life and she would just listen. They have all departed this life except for Aunt Atherstine and Aunt Geneva. They both sing like birds and each has claimed to be the one that will attend the other's funeral. I really didn't get to know Yancine.

My Uncle Dwight rode me on his Bike handle bars as a kid and guided my path in life after the death of my dad. He once told me the story of a man that was waiting on God because he was stuck on his house's rooftop because the flood water in his city had risen to the level of the roof. Anyway, two boats and a helicopter came by to rescue him, and he said an emphatically "No" to all three rescuers. He told them that he was simply waiting on God. The flood waters increased and eventually drown him. He got to heaven and asked God why had he let him die and God said, "Who do you think sent the helicopter and two boats!" In other words, sometimes God is speaking to us through people and we ignore him while yet simultaneously claiming we want to hear from him.

My dad was also a minister and my Uncle Dwight was an attorney and a medical doctor that often spoke like a minister. There were only 200 attorney/doctors in the United States at this time and he was one of them. After the death of my dad, a deep void was created in my life, it would be my Uncle Dwight that would both hurt me and yet help me like no one else in my life. He would pick up the baton left by my dad's departure and fill up the void in my life and school me about the intricacies and complexities of life, but he would also hurt me. He once told me that some people in the family don't like you, but I think it is because they don't know you. He also told me that members of our family were either at the extreme of brilliant or crazy and that there were no in between family member.

My Uncle Dwight James, Sr. is no longer here today, but he is surely missed. He passed away in November of 2018. He was an excellent doctor and a very smart lawyer. He was very quick witted and quite funny. He was also a great orator. He was simply a Giant of a Man, both physically and mentally. He often made me laugh and even cracked me up on many occasions when he talked about various people. He often saw life from a different perspective and saw what others simply didn't see in life. He once told me that a man's politics were left of Farrakhan. I thought that was so funny that he thought anyone could be left of Farrakhan.

I asked him after graduating from college whether I should I go to law school or get a job. He said I could go to law school for three years or sit on the corner for the next three years. He said time was simply neutral and it does not care about my choices in life. He often said that since time was neutral that time did not care if we waste our life away or got up and went to school. He said time would still turn, the Sun and the Moon would still shine, whether we did something constructive with our life or even if we choose to just stand on the corner and do nothing with our lives. Time would still move forward with or without us. This advice impressed me immensely and so I enrolled in law school.

He also taught me to compartmentalize problems by putting them on a shelf and dealing with them later when I was ready. In short, make your problems manageable rather than overwhelming. I often tell my students if you have any problems to tell your problems that I must take an Exam right now and I will deal with you later after I finish studying for my Exam.

He was also like a Bank to me; he would often loan me money and frequently simply just gave me money. He would ask me to serve a lawsuit which is normally $65 dollars, but he would give me $500 to do the service. He would also give me $500, $600, or $1000 to do work for him. He would say type up this paperwork and usually the paperwork cost $50 or $60 dollars and yet he would overpay me with $500 or a thousand. He gave me gifts, loans, forgave me of debts and hired me to work in my first job after law school as his law clerk. I went around bragging to everyone that I worked for a doctor and a lawyer. It was blatant nepotism, but I wasn't complaining because I had my foot in the door of the legal field and I had my own office space, first on prestigious Wilshire in Los Angeles and later in Downtown Los Aneles on Grand Avenue. He gave me my own office and he was considered of counsel to the prestigious law firm.

I once owed him $700 and he told me that if I helped him

move furniture from his office to a truck that I could keep the $700 loan and I went to help him move and he cancelled repayment of the loan. He gave me encouragement and directed my life like a director on a movie set directs actors. I missed being able to call Dr James or Uncle Dwight as I would affectionally called him. I miss his wise counsel and medical advice and even medications. He taught me what foods to eat and what foods to avoid in order to stay healthy and the pros and cons of each medication he prescribed to me. He often referred me all the legal business that he did not want to handle in life.

I remember once he had a conflict in his two businesses of medicine and law, so he sent me up north to do a deposition. Here I am a mere paralegal and he paid me to go up North and act like an attorney. I went up North and told the attorneys, who had never seen him, that I was Dwight. Years later I would apply for a job and one of the attorneys on the hiring committee in Southern,-California said to me, "I have seen you somewhere before" I said, "I have never seen you before." He subsequently hired me to work for his law firm. I never told him that I was the guy impersonating Uncle Dwight up North at the deposition years before and he never figured it out or if he did then he never said anything.

My uncle Dwight married outside of his race while in college. He had two beautiful kids, Raquel and Charlene and a lovely wife named Kathy. My dad always ridiculed Dwight for marrying outside his race. He told him that Samson dated outside his race and it was his downfall. However, Uncle Dwight kept a poker face and took it all in stride.

He taught English at the University of Wyoming while simultaneously attending law school. His first wife Kathy worked hard to help him get through school. One of my paternal cousins, James Ray, took his English class and was sitting way in the back of the classroom with other black students on the first day of English class. James Ray said that my Uncle Dwight told all the black students in the back corner that it was very dark in the corner back there, and they picked up the hint and dispersed and moved up to the front of the class.

Uncle Dwight told me his dad Elijah used to take him to the hospital to watch surgeries because Dwight said he wanted to be a doctor. Also, he told me that when he left Cheyenne, Wyoming and moved back to California that he had not seen so many beautiful black women in his life. He told me when he was at the grocery store, he would sometimes just stare because black women in Cheyenne were sparse but there were so many beautiful black women in California.

He moved back to California to get his medical degree at the University of Irvine and it was there that he met a black medical student named Beverly. The two of them would have a platonic friendship that lasted for years. He told me that he would of married Beverly but she ran out of the house when they had an argument one time and went to a motel with a complete stranger that she picked up on the corner and she had sex with the stranger. They remained friends but he said would never marry her.

At Dwight's graduation from medical school, in 1978, I would meet a medical student named Gail and date her while I was in law school. She and Beverly were real good friends. My uncle was shocked that I was able to pull Gail at his graduation party and could not believe it when I told him I had her phone number. After the party, Robbie, my cousin, had tried to talk to her too, but I was the one that came away with her number and it really surprised him because Robbie had the reputation of being a Mack Daddy while I was just considered to be studious.

My Uncle Dwight was always trying to get rich quickly. He tried gambling in vain, working with the Russian Mafia in vain. Then working with the Italian Mafia and even Black gangsters; but success would not come to him until he finally settled down and started going to church. Once he met his second wife, Yolanda, and started to do the will of God, he let the other distractions in life go, and established four of his own medical clinics in Riverside, Porterville, Inglewood, and San Jose and that is when he finally made a lot of money. His house in Riverside was a Mansion.

Much of his success was due to a young patient named Yolanda that came to his office one day and stole his heart. He told me initially that he had no intentions of getting married again, but she melted his heart. He had picked a Plum out of the Tree of Life. He would have two more kids by her, Dwight Jr and Nikki, and then he adopted Yolanda's son, Joey, as his son, and he would stay with her for the remaining days of his life. She was instrumental in him turning around his life and giving his life balance.

His presence is surely missed these days. He was wise and witty beyond his age and helped so many people with medicine, weight loss, health issues, diabetes along with loans and gifts and legal issues. He gave seminars on health issues and was a doctor to movie stars as well. He often gave family get togethers, BBQ's, and had meals catered for his large family. He had triumphs and tragedies and yet he always rebounded in life.

Dwight lived to be 70, my dad would die at 46. He was the wisest man I would ever meet in life. We took trips together to Ridgecrest, Bishop, and Las Vegas. One time we had to go visit a bitter client of whom Dwight had loss his case. The family was irate that the client was sent to jail for molesting a patient. Dwight asked me to come with him to explain the loss to the family. Some of them threaten to jump on him, but the presence of us both made them change their mind. My Uncle Dwight once said to me "If the whole world were destroyed by a nuclear catastrophe that the only ones that would survive would be the rats and you." He knew that I would of took a bullet for him and that is why he took me over the client's house.

His life inspired others to go to school and become doctors and nurses. He would inspire people to open businesses, and many have proclaimed him as the best doctor in the world. His premature and untimely death shook up many and his absence has left a void in my life as well as countless others.

I realize now that my Uncle Dwight did so much for me to make up for some wrongs that he had done to me earlier in life. He more than paid for any wrongs that he did to me in life and I will forever treasure our relationship and will miss his presence until the day I die. He was truly one of a kind.

# Chapter 12

## SCIENCE TEACHER ERNEST

My 9th grade Science Teacher tried to engage me in homosexual acts. I received A's in his class and won student of the month at Eastern Junior High. My parents bought me a microscope that same year because I said one day that I wanted to be a doctor. My science teacher initially gave me rides home from school as I sought his advice on girls in my classes and then eventually, we would stop at his house in route to my house. My stepdad John never liked him at all.

When I told Ernest that this fine girl in class didn't like me. He told me that I was aiming too high. He told me to date ugly girls first and then build up my confidence. I followed his advice and as my confidence grew in life the finer were the women I would approach and win to a courtship. I realized that the veneer between ugly and pretty is very thin and emotions override looks. In other words, ugly women like to hear the same thing as beautiful women. I learned that ugly women like compliments just like pretty woman and that compliments will melt their hearts just like any glamorous woman.

I once told my son what I had learn from Ernest and told them when they were younger to date ugly women and all three of them laughed at me and said, "no way." I just smiled.

I would later in life approach more attractive women as I got older with boldness and confidence, but all that confidence came from initially talking to ugly women. I came to realize that beauty is only skin deep, and I came to realize that some glamorous women had real depth of character and others were very shallow. They both like compliments and I would gain an Encyclopedia of knowledge from dating ugly chicks. Women are the same, whether they are ugly or beautiful, certain words will melt their hearts.

The thing that I didn't like about Ernest is that he started telling me in the car that his penis was hurting. On several rides home, he would finally pull it out and play with it while he was driving. I thought it was weird but ignored him until one day he asked me to suck it. I refused to suck it and he got upset initially and then said subsequently it was okay, but what shocked me was all the people he claimed to have had sex with at the school. He told me he was having sex with one of the top teachers in the school and the names of other students that had obliged him.

That would not be the last time I had an encounter with homosexuality, I would learn as I aged that it was very prevalent in our African American community and many closet homosexuals would eventually come out of the closet as I aged in life. Many of them hid their sexual preference and secretly hit on young school children. I never succumbed to his wishes and eventually I left Pontiac to go live in Long Beach with my dad. Years later, after I got out of the Army, I went back to Pontiac Michigan to visit my parents and saw him again. While we were sitting in his living room, he again pulled out his penis and asked me would I play with it. I responded by pulling out my own penis and said I will play with it if you suck mine. Those words alone made him put his penis back in his pants and he never asked me again. I think that teenager he once met was now a man and he treated me that way from that day forward.

I realize now that Ernest was bisexual. but the teacher that I looked up to at that time in my life was Mr. Nelson. Mr. Nelson also taught at Eastern Jr. High and he had a black wife and a white mistress and they both knew about each other and yet they both loved him. I thought that was out of this world and I wanted to be like Mr. Nelson and not like Ernest as a youngster.

Later in life, Ernest unsuccessfully tried marriage to a woman. His broke all the dishes because his wife would not wash dishes, He refused to admit that he was a genuine homosexual and his futile attempts at a heterosexual lifestyle simply did not work.

I even took his wife out to lunch one day and was thoroughly convinced their relationship was over. She was more interested in white men than in him. He also came to visit my wife and I in Long Beach one day. I recall that I went to buy some weed on Orange St in Long Beach and the guy took my money but didn't come back with any weed. I went home to get my gun to go kill him over $25, but Ernest talked me out of seeking revenge and gave me the $25 dollars that I had lost. He felt and I also realize now that Black people often kill each other over trivia matters and my killing him over $25 dollars' worth of weed was senseless and would only change the course of my life and land me in jail. Once he gave me the $25 dollars that I had loss I calmed down.

That would be the last time that I would see him. Later in life, he would disappear, and I would never hear from him again.

# Chapter 13

## WHITE MEN IN PONTIAC, MICHIGAN

One day when I was about 14 years old, my mom sent me to mail a letter rather late at night. The mailbox was only a couple blocks from my home. My street started out straight and then curved like the letter J, and as I headed toward the curve portion of the street, I heard the noise of neighborhood kids yelling to three white men that were having sex with black prostitutes in an abandoned home to get out of our neighborhood and simultaneously throwing rocks at the abandoned house while they were allegedly performing their sexual acts.

Along comes me, not a part of the dispute, innocent, and simply following my mom's instructions to mail a letter.

After I mailed the letter and as I am returning to my home, I looked back and see this white man running down the street and suddenly, un-expectantly, and surprisingly, he grabs me by the neck and jacket and starts to beat me and then his two friends soon come along and join in on the melee. They proceeded to call me the "N" words and heap fists upon fists on my body and face, while one of them holds me tight from behind. I try to unzip my front zipped jacket that they are now holding from behind and slip away; hoping to leave them holding the jacket, but to no avail. One white man quips we got a smart one! At the same time, the neighborhood kids are yelling, "Let him go, he didn't do anything", as the three men start leading me back to the house where they had been ; but their impotent cries for them to let me go fell on deaf ears.

Finally, after a few minutes of this one-sided beating, and my feeble attempt at an escape, a man walks out on his front porch and says, in a loud voice, "Let him go-now! "They tell him to get back in the house "Nigger" and mind your business. He goes back in the house and grabs a shotgun and comes back out and shoots it in the air and those white men immediately let me go. I took off running to my house in the opposite direction because I didn't want them to know where I lived.

I found out later that the guy that fired the shotgun was a cocaine dealer and he was later arrested by the police for dealing cocaine out of his very own restaurant. Despite what he was, on that day, he saved my life. My mom called the police and the police said they couldn't do anything because the three white men said the neighborhood kids and I had started the incident and therefore no charges were ever filed and that is why I went into the law to fight against those types of injustices.

The second time I experience blatant racism was in Orange county, as I was able to hustle up enough change so that my starving law student butt could sit down at a bus bench to eat some McDonald's food ; a white man pulled up to the bus stop and call me a "Nigger" and as he proceeded to drive off ; I, although very hungry, foolishly, threw all my food and drink at his car as he sped away. I learned from that incident never to throw food at white people, especially when you are hungry because I had nothing to eat afterwards and I watched as multiple cars drove over my food while my stomach ached.

Those of you who say the "N" word has no meaning and that it is neutral really don't know what you are talking about. Those of you who say the meaning is simply subjective, have forgot the objectivity of the word. Do not ever tell me that the word exists in a vacuum, the word is vile, humiliating, and disparaging, it was birthed during the evils of slavery and has its roots in the emasculation of freed slaves. It was born in evil, it is an evil word, and those of you who use it cavalier and nonchalantly, truly do not understand the meaning and the history of the word.

The third time I encountered blatant racism, my wife walked to the store one day and a bunch of roofers in Fullerton in Orange County called her that vile name and I honestly can't tell you what I did afterwards and I hope she never does. They didn't say it again.

I hate the word, its history, semantics, and etymology. I have seen it used under the vilest and most contemptible circumstances and I will always despise the word and never use it to describe a friend, family member, or acquaintances. It does not mean my buddy, my homie, my friend, to me. The word means hate and those who used it on each other truly do not understand what they are saying. It is not a neutral word, you cannot take a word that many black man and women, who hung from trees, heard as the last word in their life, or the kids bombed in churches, or dragged out of home, or murdered on highways, or killed for looking at a southern white woman heard.

Just because many young artists and young people have money does not give them the right to make the word vogue or fashionable to use. Those of you, who do use it, truly do not understand what you are saying to each other. You are actually saying the white man' s opinion of you is also your opinion of you. Nothing could be further from the truth.

You will never hear me say it nor have I heard my sons or daughter saying it. If you want to say it, be my guest, but you will never say it in my house, or on my fb page or in my life! I contest the word in its original form as well as its variations.

There is a verse in scriptures that says the power of life and death is in the tongue, Proverbs 18:21 to be exact. We can speak life to people's life or even death. Words do have power and they are not neutral. I prefer to be called women, women of God, and Men, men of God, or doctor, to me those words are uplifting, and they identify you with something positive and meaningful. My words say you count, you matter, and God loves you!

# Chapter 14

## Long Beach Poly High School

After leaving Eastern Jr. High School, I started the 10th grade at Pontiac Central High School and then went to a parochial school called Pontiac Catholic and then finally I went to live with my dad and attended Long Beach Poly High School. My memories of Pontiac Central were that we took the State Championship in Basketball that year. We won because of a phenomenal athlete named Campy Russell. I also remember walking out of my class as Black Students walked out to protest the treatment we were receiving in the school. I was in one of the advanced college preparatory class at Pontiac Central with only a few other Afro Americans. The White Teacher said if you guys want to join them then you can join the walk out. I got up out of my chair and walked out of the class, but all the other Afro Americans stayed put in their seat.

Then my parents transferred me to Pontiac Catholic which was a very rigid school. I started running Track and going out with a white girl name Theresa in those days. She basically ran her whole house. She actually told her parents that she was dating a black guy and there was nothing they could do about it. We never had sex, but I spent many days over her house watching television, eating food, and playing games and occasionally we would kiss.

My stepdad and I were now clashing more frequently in those days and so I decided to leave Michigan and move back to California and attend Long Beach Poly High, which was across the street from Roosevelt Elementary, the school I attended in the 4th grade.

When I arrived in Long Beach, my dad was so excited that he took me by all his family members house in the middle of the night. He was probably saying my dad Elijah said they would come back and look the first one is here. I am sure my Aunts were annoyed that he was waking them up in the middle of the night, but no one said anything to him.

Once in Long Beach, I went to school called Long Beach Polytechnic High. There was no school like Long Beach Poly. It was a Cosmopolitan school of every ethnicity that you could ever imagine in life. Asians, Mexicans, Africans, Europeans, were all getting along and learning.

Then one day despite all that harmony, a racial riot broke out in the Quad Area with about 500 students fighting in April of 1972. Apparently, mistreatment of Blacks at a movie theater had spread to the campus. It seemed to me that as soon as they took the police car from in front of the school that the riots broke out.

Prior to the racial riot, I primarily was engaged in the sports of cross country and track. I could run the 2 miles in 10 minutes and 30 seconds and my best time in the 600 meters was 1 minutes and 29 seconds. I also ran the 400 meters and the 800 meters. The athletes that I trained with at Poly in those days were Jeff Haynes and Elvie Howard. Jeff Haynes would later go to Long Beach City College and win the State Championship in the 800 meter and then run track for UCLA. Elvie would be my teammate that I could never beat in running the 800 meters.

He would even beat me in the workouts on the practice field at Poly. I had heard of Elvie before he came to Poly. While he was at Stephens Junior High School, he had run the 600 meters in 1: 26. A phenomenal time for a ninth grader.

We were on the same track team with speedsters like Leonard Ross, who would one day run the 100-yard dash in 9.6 and Ricky Ivy, 9.7 along with James Warren and Tony Brown. We also had a high hurdle phenom named James Royal and a 400-meter phenom named Sam Hill. Tony Brown would one day jump over 26 feet in the long jump, a record that still stands 49 years later at Long Beach Poly High. Carl Miles, who we called Tucker. would one day high jump 6'10" inches. It was as if all the stars were in alignment for that track team.

I also ran cross country with Nathan Richardson, who would later become a lawyer and was shot in his law office in 1989 and I also ran with Richard Simmons, a world traveler, along with Joseph Prevo.

One moment at Poly I will never forget was when I went to sit at a lunch table in the Cafeteria and this big guy named David, was sitting with a host of other athletes and popular kids. He said, "Chumps cannot sit at this table." I was new at Long Beach Poly High, having recently transferred from Pontiac Catholic and I replied, "Then why are you sitting here?"

We both exchanged harsher words, mostly from me, talking about his mom being on the Aunt Jemimah Pancake Box while I was still sitting at the table. I calmly ate my food while sitting there and was acting with bravado, but inside I was really scared. We now call it selling wolf cookies. However, I refused to let him embarrass me in front of all his fellow athletes and friends, He was popular in the school and was a huge 200 pound or more basketball player and I was a virtual unknown skinny 120 pound new kid on the block.

After I finished eating my food, he told me that he was going to catch me and beat me up. I told him that he was too big and slow to catch me which only angered him even more. I slowly walked away from the table after eating my food and dump my tray and walked away but I was never comfortable because I always felt he was around the corner. I kept looking over my shoulder in fear and trepidation and was prepared to run if he came near me. Everywhere I went I was constantly turning my head wondering if he was around the corner or behind me. He told me that he was going to beat me up and I believed him.

Then one day he cornered me in the track stadium seats. The track stadium looked like a section of a Roman amphitheater. I ran up to the top portion while he was at the bottom to avoid him, but he pursued me. Then out of nowhere my cousin Monte showed up. Monte was one of the baddest dude in Long Beach at the time and he had an infamous reputation for beating up people. He was short but yet muscular and quick. He could beat up people twice his sizes and his reputation for not taking shit was well known and last but not least-he was my cousin. He had been in several fights and always won because he was so quick with his fists. I explained to Monte about my fears of David as David came nearer toward me. Monte walked over to David and said something to David and he simply walked away and never chased me again. When we would see each other from that day forward, we would speak and say hi to each other. We never became close friends, but he always showed me respect and I never again feared him chasing me Monte never told me what he said to him, but his mere presence as my cousin saved me from what would have definitely been a one sided beating that day.

I also remember Carl Miles, he jumped a 6 ft 10 inches in the high jump, on the track team telling me that I was a sorry athlete and I replied," I may be sorry, but I get more pussy than you do."

He was so angry at my comment that my teammates had to hold him back. I realized at an early age that I couldn't physically beat some of these guys in high school but my wit was much quicker than theirs and my mouth, which I was told later in life is the gift of Gab, was getting me in and out of trouble. I was very quick witted, and I could think fast on my feet and therefore my mouth in life would be both a blessing and a curse. It would often get me out of trouble as well as into trouble.

I also remember in high school that I used Monte's name to get my leather coat back from another nonathlete named Ricky. Ricky stole my Leather Coat out of my gym locker while I was running Track. The reason I found out was because Carl told me, and I confronted Ricky about the theft. Ricky feigned ignorance of the theft and said, "I don't know what you are talking about." I said to him. "That that leather coat you stole did not belong to me but rather it was my cousin Monte's." I said, "If you do not bring that Leather Jacket back to me tomorrow then I am going to tell Monte you stole his leather coat, because if I do not bring it back to him, then he will beat me up and I will not take a beating from him for something you did, you better have that Leather Coat here tomorrow morning or I am going to tell him that you took it. "He said, "I don't know what you are talking about". But the next day, he brought the leather coat to school and said I found it on the way to school. I said I know you did. That was actually my leather coat and not Monte's. It showed me that I could use my brain and mouth to get things in life and that I did not have to resort to violence.

God gives each of us something to get out of the ghettos of life. Some of us are basketball players, other are baseball players and actors and then some of us are just thinkers with the gift of Gab. Always use your gift to excel in life.

One of the saddest moments in my life was when my girlfriend

Kathy was raped in High school and several men ran a train on her. She was my girlfriend and she was hurt, and she soon moved away to Oklahoma. She was high on a drug we called REDS back in those days. She could not identify the guys because she was high, but I always felt it was guys at my Poly High School.

I would run into other women that had been raped later in my life as well. Betty was raped at a bus stop in Los Angeles at knife point and she was forced to get in a car and Gail was raped by a man that said her tire was low and to follow him to a gas station and then forced her to get in his car and took her to his house and raped her repeatedly. I hate rapists to this day, and they will never receive any sympathy from me.

My best friend in High School in those days was Olen. He was on the track team with me and our relationship was essentially a love/hate relationship. My dad told me that he was not a good friend, but I refused to listen to my dad. I would find out years later that my dad was right on point about many things in life. He simply had a sixth sense.

One time Olen and I were at the beach making love to two different girls and I said lets switch and we switched partners while making love on the beach in the sand and I couldn't believe the girls agreed to the switch but such was life in Long Beach in those High School days.

Olen and I were also with some girls in the car one time and they wouldn't sleep with us. Olen pulled over the car and made them get out. I said that is not right and I got out of the car with the ladies and walked them both homes. Olen drove off. I liked Olen but some of his ways troubled me.

I also ran away from Home while in the 12$^{th}$ grade in Long Beach. I ran away from home because my Dad was not treating me right. He made me come home from school in the middle of the day because he heard I wore my brother's shoes to school.

I said to him couldn't you have waited until I got home, and he said he wanted to address it now. So, in the middle of the day I had to catch the bus to come home to change shoes and then I went back to school. I left home shortly thereafter and came back home because I did not have anywhere to go the first time, but the second time, I ran away because of how he treated my stepmother Gloria and never came back.

My first runaway was spontaneous and unsuccessful but the second one was well planned out. I got tired of my stepmom Gloria getting beat at night in the bedroom and having to listen to her cries. Her cries came through the walls of my bedroom which was adjacent to theirs. I planned my second escape carefully and went to stay with my cousin, once removed, Jackie,

I also went on the television show called Soul Train with girls from Saint Anthony High School during this time. Carol Larue had heard about my ability to dance and invited me on the show with her friend Sheila. I tried to hit on Sheila, but she had a crush on Ricky Ivy on our track team and let me know immediately that I was wasting my time pursuing her. I threw in the towel. Soul Train was a great experience and I was able to meet Don Cornelius and other entertainers.

In high school, I did some really crazy things. I once asked my girlfriend Kathy to have sex with my brother Othello and she said Okay. She made love to him because he was in the 10th grade and had not had sex in his life. He was very appreciative of me. I told him now you know how it feels. He could not stop thanking me and I could not believe she did it, but she did. For some reason, I didn't see anything wrong with sharing my woman with my brother but that sharing would end after high school.

I also had a girlfriend named Doris in those days. I came over her house and she had a Hickey on her neck. I asked her about it, and she said a Mosquito bite her. I said That Mosquito sure had some big lips. I tried to make love to her while her parents were gone one day but could not get an erection. I looked at her innocent vagina, but I could not make entry. I could not part her Red Seas and I simply could not perform. I do not know if I were fearful that her dad would show up and catch us or if I overly respected her. I once told her that it was the moment of my life that I often regret and we both just smile. She is a successful executive these days.

A unique guy came to Long Beach Poly High School while I was there from Alabama. His name was James Johnson. He ran for the student body President and won. He was an outsider that came to Long Beach Poly and won President of Student Body at Long Beach Poly overwhelmingly. He was a confident brother at a young age, and he challenged a white boy for the presidency and handsomely beat him. We were so happy to have one of us as the student body President. He would later work for Sesame Street Television Series on Television and then joined the Army and later become a city employee for Long Beach. I always thought he would have been a great politician, but he never did - such is life.

My cousin Robbie and I ran away from home and we meet some girls at the Pike. The Pike was a big circus that was stationary rather than transitory. We went to Robbie 's sister house to party with the girls in San Pedro. Once Robbie fell to sleep. His girl and I started kissing in the bathroom. When Robbie woke up, I told him his girl had been unfaithful. Not realizing that I had also been unfaithful. She said that I was a lying ass and Robbie believed her. I learn from that day forward to keep my mouth shut. Her denial was more convincing than my truth. I learned later in life that she was a prostitute in Hollywood.

However, Robbie would pay me back later. After I was married, I left the house to go party one night by myself. I told Robbie

I was going to party. When I came home, he was sleeping on my couch pretending to be dead sleep. My wife said he and his woman had a fight and he came over the house to get away from her. I actually believed her at the time.

I realized he had sex with her and sleeping on the couch was a pretense to throw me off. You live and learn. My cousin Monte would also score with her. He was over my house as soon as I went to school in those days. I do not blame them. If a woman is voluntarily giving up sex why not milk the cow. Neither one of them force her and I would soon divorce her.

My ex-wife told my present wife, Jacqueline, that you can lie to him because he will believe anything you tell him. That is what I got for being trusting with my first wife. I am so glad that I left her quick, fast, and in a hurry.

Many of my friends told me they didn't like my new wife because if I wasn't home, then she didn't let family or friends in our house. My friends told me we do not like her at all. She would tell them you are Hudena's friend and he is not home. What a blessing- finally a loyal, faithful wife and 40 years later and we are still together.

In high school, Brady had an apartment that he allowed people to come over to and gamble. You had to pay the house to get in and you could gamble for money. Brady often betted on me in the stands as I ran track. He would later get two girls pregnant in high school and afterwards commit some crimes that would land him in prison. He had great leadership skills that were never realized. He should be the executive of a large corporation because he had natural leadership skills but wasted talent in the ghettoes of America is a proverb.

He would often tease me about a girl that I was dating named Kathy and let me know brothers were trying to take her from me.

I remember Johnny borrowed his car to go to the Poly prom

and wrecked it. I remember saying I am glad that I did not wreck his car.

While I was at Roosevelt, President Kennedy was shot, I was crying with most of the kids and some white guy at school said now that Kennedy is dead, they are going to send all black people back to Africa. I can remember crying profusely that I do not want to go to Africa. Please do not send us to Africa and once I got home my dad assured me it was not happening.

Art Henry aka Hank sent me to deliver some vending machine out of state. While driving the trucks across state lines this white boy said over the Citizen Band Radio aka the CB Radio," Does anyone see any Niggers on the road?" I got on the CB Radio and told the white boy that you cannot even speak English properly and that I speak your language better than you do. I could not believe how angry those words made him. He was literally crying on the CB radio telling other Truckers on the radio, "Did any Trucker see that Nigger.... does anyone see that Nigger? He said," I am going to kill that kill that Nigger" I was laughing on the CB Radio. This was my gift. The gift of gab!

I could talk men into giving me money and I could talk woman into giving money and even pussy. I could not jump as high Carl. I could not run as fast as Leonard. I could not beat Elvie in the 800 or jump as long as Tony, but no one had the gift of Gab like me. I realize that one day. I could not fight like Othello and Monte. My gift was quite different. It was simply the gift to outthink and out strategies my opponents in life and I would use that gift for the rest of my life in order to succeed in life.

Another funny thing I saw in life at an early age was that there were firecrackers in life that thought they were dynamite and dynamite with low self-esteem that thought they are firecracker. I even remember on the radio Snoop Dog saying he like girls with low self-esteem. One of the most important things in life that I would learn is that your perception of your self can determine your fate.

Another person that came in my life during the days at Poly was my Uncle Robert also affectionately known as Butchie. Butchie was my maternal Uncle and my mom's brother and he would often pick us up on some weekends and take us to Pomona to party with other teenagers. Butchie picked up Othello and I along with my cousin Charles Lakey and we all often went to the Teen Center in Pomona to party. The three of us would often party together in Pomona and even go to Compton back in those days. Dancing and chasing skirts were so much fun in those days.

# Chapter 15

## Army

I finally graduated from high school in June of 1972 and immediately joined the Army. I left the getting high group in high school in June of 1972 to join the Army in July of 1972. I would later leave the Army group to attend college in 1975 and then leave the college group to attend law school in 1978. Sometimes in life, we must leave a group of people in order to progress in life.

I joined the Army because I was disgusted with my life and what was becoming of it. I walked into a laundromat one day and snatched a lady's purse that was on a table while she was putting her clothes from the dryer into the basket. She screamed so loud and said, "Please Mister, Please Mister, do not take my purse." The sound of her screams was piercing to my ears and I felt her cries in my heart and dropped her purse. I realize that a life of crime was just not for me. The next day I joined the Army.

The teachings of my mom and dad would resonate with me for the rest of my life. I felt that if I gave the Army 3 years of my life that they would give me 4 years of college. The idea of climbing out of the poor class to the middle class was simply overwhelming and I signed on the dotted line. I took them up on that opportunity to sacrifice three years of my life for 4 years of college. While I was in the Army, I found out that you could also go to college at night for free and it did not count toward your 4 years of college benefits once you got out. I went to school for one year and a half while stationed in Fort Leonard Wood, Missouri and would later transfer those units to CSULB. Now I could have the VA educational benefits for just 2.5 years of college and apply the 1.5 years of benefits to law school. Then they gave Viet Nam Veterans an extra year of benefits and I was able to apply 2.5 years of VA Benefits to 3 years of law school. This was my opportunity to move on up and I could not pass it up. The major lesson that I learned from the Army was self-discipline and staying focused in pursuit of your goals in life.

While I was in the Army, I tried to maintain my relationship with my high school girlfriend and so we sent tapes in lieu of letters to each other. We thought listening to an actual voice would keep us together longer than dry and insipid letters. I meet my first wife in high school. She was pursued by several men, but I won her heart. We tried to keep the relationship together for 3 years with personal visits, tape recordings of each other's voice and picture and letters.

However, one day she called me with only 6 months left to go on my 3 year Army Tour of Duty and confessed that she had cheated on me with another man and the other man had told her she should confess to me her indiscretions. My ego simply would not let her go and I told her that I forgave her. We later married and had one son and broke up immediately thereafter. I told my dad that she was a Rose and he told me that Roses had thorns and I would never be able to get rid of those thorns. I told him that I would just cut off the thorns and he just stared at me. I regret not listening to my dad.

My first wife's father once told me that he could not believe I had joined the White Man's Army and I replied, "Someone must do the fighting. Not everyone can run from the war. Some men must stand up and fight. We all can't run." He just stared at me and didn't say nothing. He had a reputation for hitting my first wife's sister's boyfriend, but he never put his hands on me. I realize now that I was young, cocky, and confident and had no filters.

After seeing my high school girlfriend off, I headed to my first encounter with Sergeant Norvell. Sgt Norvell was my Drill Sergeant in Basic Training at Fort Ord. He was as mean as a Junkyard dog while I was stationed in Fort Ord, California. However, he took a liking to me and immediately made me a squad leader.

As a squad leader, you get to order men around. I remember marching my unit over to the chow line to eat dinner. I told everyone to stand at Parade Rest, which essentially means you stand still with both hands joined together behind your back in a relaxed attention stance. This White guy from Mississippi had no respect for my position and refused to put his hands behind his back and stand at a relaxed attention stance. The white guy simply refused and I as the new Squad Leader demanded he come to parade rest and he again refused. I started taking off my equipment gear backpack and he asked me what I was doing. I said I am talking my stuff off to kick your ass. It was only then that he came to parade rest in the chow line.

I learned from that moment forward that sometimes in life you must back your words up with actions. Telling this guy from down south to come to parade rest in chow line was not enough. I needed to back it up with action.

After 8 weeks of Basic training, I finally left the Fort Ord Base and got to visit the city of Monterey Bay. Monterey Bay Jazz Festival was held there, and I was so horny and eager to have a first experience with a prostitute. I went in the downtown area looking for a prostitute with the rest of the fellows in my squad. I slept with my first prostitute at 18 years old. I never knew white prostitutes cost more than black prostitutes up until that time. I thought they were all treated equally. I felt that I had really led a sheltered life and the real world was so different from the world I was taught to believe in. Immorality that was frowned on by the church and society ran rampant in real life.

One-time Sergeant Norvell was bragging on me and told other sergeants that I could beat anyone in the battalion in long distance running. Some other sergeants betted him on the race. They had me run against this White guy from another platoon. They had us both run for miles in the hills of Fort Ord. We both ran into those hills huffing and puffing trying to show we were the better runner and during the second mile I left him in the dust. I remember the event well because when I came out of those mountains my entire Platoon was shouting my name and cheering me on. Even one of the drill sergeant for the other side that lost the bet took me to the side and said how did you learn how to run like that and also told me that I belong in college and not the Army. My drill sergeant went to everyone collecting his money as if saying I told you guys, he was fast. I realized that running cross country in high school at Poly and running against Elvie and Jeff in High School had actually prepared me well for Army Life. No one in my Battalion could beat me running.

After Basic training in Fort Ord, I then went to Fort Sam Houston In San Antonio, Texas to be trained as a medic. I actually thought that I would be a doctor someday. San Antonio was scary in 1972, all we did is smoke weed, play cards, and talk about our life when we were at home. They warned us that if we were ever caught with a bag of weed outside of the base that the State of Texas would send us to jail for life, so everyone just smoked on base. I loved training to be a medic at 18 years old. We all thought we were headed to Viet Nam, but I never got those orders. I really loved being a 18 year old private and "Medic" in the U.S. Army.... it is one of the best decisions that I have ever made in my life.... they paid for my college education and my law school and also helped me buy my first house......I followed in after my dad and my daughter and son have followed in after me and they both currently outrank me.. My daughter is a E7 aka as a Sergeant First Class and my son is a Warrant Officer and Pilot. My daughter has been in the Army longer, but she has to salute her brother because he outranks her and they both outrank me. I was just an E4 also known as a Corporal or Specialist.

In January of 1973, I was stationed in Fort Leonard Wood, Missouri, as an Army Medic, and I was assigned to work in the General Leonard Wood Army Community Hospital, on the 5th floor ward. I saw the first death in my life when one of my elderly patients died. I had never seen actual death transpire before. I only knew about it in the abstract until that moment.

One day a male registered nurse rushed into the hospital room while I was cleaning up a patient and said, rather urgently, "Private James, we need you to run down to X-ray right now and get a "fallopian tube" for the doctor. It is Urgent because he needs to operate."

I, a mere 18 years old, and naive as the day is long, went to X-ray and asked for a fallopian tube. X-ray, being in on the joke, sent me to the Emergency Room and the Emergency room, in turn, sent me to the Surgery ward ; until finally someone pulled me to the side and said they were actually playing a joke on me.

I got back to the ward and everyone was laughing. I learned what a fallopian tube was on that day. Wow, was my only response!!

The first white girl I dated in the Army was a white girl named Kathy. I had dated a Kathy in high school and now I was dating a Kathy in the army. She was tall and slender and had long blonde hair and wore jeans with holes in them long before it became fashionable. I first saw her while I was eating lunch at the Mess Hall on the Army Base. While I was at a bench table eating my food, she suddenly appeared across the large lunchroom in a long line and simply stood out. I said to myself I would sure like to meet her one day and yet dismissed the thought as if that is something that will never happen.

I was living off base at that time in a trailer park by myself. That night, my next door neighbor, Perry, knocked on my door and told me he was trying to talk to one girl at his place and she brought her friend along and would I come keep the friend company while he talked to his intended target. I went over there to help him and got the surprise of my life. To my surprise was the white girl I had seen in the lunch line that very day in the mess hall. I talked to her for a minute and then asked her to go back to my trailer and then after drinks and weed, the inevitable happened and we made love. She told me that her boyfriend had left her to go home visit his parents during the holidays She said she felt abandoned by him. I was rewarded for giving her a sympathetic ear. However, as soon as he got back from vacation, she returned to him immediately. He and I would then compete for her attention for months until I finally won.

However, she wanted endogamy in marriage and insisted that her kids have blue eyes and I said it did not really matter and eventually we broke up. She was really confused, however, one night after we broke up, she came by the house and we had sex and because it was so cold, I gave her my leather coat to wear as she left my place. I thought I could go to her Barracks on base at Fort Leonard Wood where she now lived and get it back. The next day, she said I am not giving it back to you and her mood had totally changed. I went in the Barracks and went to her room and took it. She was appalled and told the commanding officer and he, the colonel, called me into his office for an appointment and asked me to give the leather coat back to her. I told him I am not giving her what is mine and he realized that he couldn't make me and dismissed me from his office.

She also told me that while we were together that other enlisted men would put cream in their coffee and say to her that we are lightening up this Black Nigger. They never said anything to me, but often confronted her about being in an interracial relationship with me behind my back.

Kathy once said to me that I had too much confidence for a man and I needed to be brought down a few notches. She said I reminded her of a Rat crawling up the back of a female Elephant and saying I am going to fuck the shit out of you. Those words made me laugh, but she would not be the last woman to tell me that I simply had too much confidence.

The next lady I dated in the Army was from Huntsville, Alabama and her name were BJ. I mean she was Ebony fine, so fine that she made clothes look good! She was so hot that she could make butter melt. Sergeants, Officers, all men wanted to date her, and I was a mere private and she, for some unknown reason, chose me over all of them.

Anyway, we became boyfriend and girlfriend, and I was waiting for her at a club one night and she walked into the club with two other guys hanging on both of her arms and came to my table where I was sitting by myself. I said, "Who are these guys?" She said, "These are my friends" I said, "What are they doing here?" She said, "I can bring whoever I want to the club, you are not my daddy. You are just my boyfriend" I said, "You are so right, and I will be right back, I am going to the restroom". I got in my car and went home! About 30 minutes later, someone was beating on the door at my house and yelling, "Who do you think you are leaving me at the club. I can have any man that I want, and no man leaves me." I answered the door and said, "I thought four was a crowd and to me a date was just two and you seem well occupied, so I just left."

I will not finish the rest of the story, but to make a long story short I gained her respect that day and she never did that again. The problem with a lot of people in life today is that they are too afraid to walk away from craziness, but life is a lot better when you tell craziness, stay right here, because I am gone. She thought she was so fine that no man could live without her and I proved her wrong.

The next lady I dated was Marcella. She and I live together when I was in the Army. A black nurse in the hospital old her I was cheating on her and she broke up with me immediately. She started messing with my good friend GG and we all became good friends. GG was good for her and he saturated her with attention. We all stayed good friend and attended parties together. I was no good for her. Prior to the breakup. She took me to meet her parents in Illinois and we were talking about marriage, but I thought it was too soon to marry. The friendship turned out to be better than the sexual relationship. She was a good catch for GG, but she was not a good catch for me. GG loved her immensely. She also told me she messed around on me with a Military Policeman during my absence from the Army Base one time.

Years later, I would be streaking through the girl's barracks. I saw college students streaking in college on television and decided I wanted to try it on the Army base. I thought for sure the girls would report me to the Captain, but I was never court martialed or called into the office. Again, no reports, no calls to the Captain's office. I knocked on the upstairs barrack's window of Heidi and told her I wanted to streak naked through the barracks. Instead of not opening the window, she opened the window and asked me to kiss her before I walked through the barracks naked.

We kissed passionately and then I walked through the barracks naked, other girls woke up other girls and they came and circled me out and talked to me and thanked me for showing up naked. I wasn't there more than 10 minutes and I thought for sure the next day that I would be court martialed, but they never called me into the office.

My relationship with these Army girls in Fort Leonard Wood were not going well so on my next visit to Long Beach, I decided to elope with my high school girlfriend and bring her back to live with me in Fort Leonard Wood. I told her lets run away and get married. She said yes and we flew back to Fort Leonard Wood. I got her a job at a Hamburger place and we settled into our new lifestyle, I thought finally we are together, and we will settle down in Fort Leonard Wood and eventually get married and raise a family. A few days later, I came home from the Army Base and sitting in my trailer park was my girlfriend's mother. My girlfriend had told her mother where we were, and her mother took her back to Long Beach. This is the second time I should of saw the writing on the wall and left her, but I didn't.

Another time, a friend of mine named Pam. was arrested by the Military Police in Fort Leonard Wood and about 25 to 30 people were outside the police station demanding her release. The police had vicious dogs that they were holding by the leash and the black people were demanding Pam's release from the police station. I walked from amongst the crowd and walked up to the sergeant in charge of the police and asked if I could at least see her to assure the others that she was okay. They let me through the police and dogs, and I visited her. She assured me she was fine. I went back and told everyone she was okay. All of them then left. I could not believe that I had settled that dispute and later I left with one of the women in that crowd and she would tell me that incident is what made her have the hots for me. I guess bravery does have its rewards.

When I was in the Army, I also hitchhiked from Fort Leonard Wood Missouri to Long Beach, California to attend my brother Othello's wedding. Many people offered me many rides along the way, but I told many of them no. I never got in a car with a male person that had several people in the car. I constantly watched the driver's hands and I was always alert. One man in a truck asked me did I want to go up in the mountains and smoke some weed and then he would drive me to California, and I said no. I may of never came out of those mountains. This black woman in a truck with her elderly mom gave me a ride for countless miles. She warned me that she had a gun. I was even about to turn back in Arizona and then this white guy headed to Irvine picked me up and brought me all the way to Long Beach, California.

My dad could not believe that I had hitchhiked and scolded me as a parent should. I never did that again, but I am here today because I was very discerning about whose car or that I rode in.

I have never told anyone this before but when I was 18 years old, back in 1972, I was arrested for possession of Marijuana. The police pulled my friend Olen and I over in Long Beach, California and put me under arrest because the weed fell out of my glove compartment when he asked for my registration.

The police turned on their lights and Olen said what do you want me to do with the weed. I said, "Put it in the glove compartment." The police asked for my license and registration and as I opened up the glove compartment, the weed fell out.

He asked me whose weed was it and I said mine. He put me under arrest and let Olen drive my car to his house.

I spent three days in jail. Once I was in jail, I said I am going to become friends with the biggest dude in here so I would have protection in the event of a fight. I went to talk to this big black guy, but his voice and mannerism made me realize he was gay. I then became a friend with this guy who was a murderer and we became good friend. I felt if he had murdered once that he probably wouldn't hesitate to murder again. On the third day, I went to see the Judge. He told me that it was good I had recently joined the Army, several months before, and that because I had joined the Army, he would drop the charges against me and also seal my record.

The Judge showed me some mercy. He granted me a pass in life. The law cannot always be rigid. It must be flexible and fair and show mercy.

I never again got in trouble with the law again for weed in Long Beach and I think that Judge for seeing something in me that day that even I did not see at the time.

While I was in Fort Leonard Wood, I kept waiting for a Marijuana bust to come but it never came. The particulars are my roommate Tommy was in the room when the officers made a surprise inspection of our rooms in the dormitory. Tommy upon hearing the door opening, threw a pound of Marijuana on my bed as he feigned to be sleep on his bed that was adjacent to mine. We had four beds in each room, but Tommy was the only one in the room at the time.

He did all this while I was down the hall taking a shower. Naturally, the officer confiscated the weed, but they never called us down for a court martial as I expected. Several weeks later, I was talking to a Nurse on the 5th Ward at the Fort Leonard Wood Hospital that was a second lieutenant and she told me that she was at a party at a Lake with other junior officers and they had unlimited weed. I realized those officers had got high off of Tommy's weed but neither of us ever got in trouble or court martialed.

I also traveled to Lincoln University in Jefferson City Missouri to party in my Army days. It was an actual Black College in the capitol of Missouri. I went there initially to see an Eddie Kendrick's concert. He had a hit called. "Keep on trucking" and he was an ex -Temptation. I would often go to Lincoln University while I was stationed in Fort Leonard Wood Missouri. The college was located in Jefferson City, Missouri, the Capital of Missouri. An 80-mile trip and I meet a young lady that lived across the street from the prison The Missouri State Penitentiary was in Jefferson City. Missouri. It was the same prison James Earl Ray escaped from in order to kill Dr. King.

The first woman I met at the college told me she was pregnant with my baby and she needed money for an abortion. Her roommate pulled me to the side and told me that she was trying to con me and that her friend hated men and was simply using me to get money and that she wasn't pregnant at all. I thank her and saved my money. The second lady I dated at Lincoln University looked like Diana Ross. She admitted to me that she liked me a lot but that she was also messing with her married professor at the college. She would see me when they were breaking up and break up with me when they were together. I decided that the relationship was not worth it and stopped going to Jefferson City, Missouri.

My brother Othello once came to visit me when I was in the Army and brought a pound of weed. I do not know how he got it on the base, but he did.

When I was in the army in the 1970's, a group of my buddies and I went to a party at the NCO club in Fort Leonard Wood, Missouri.

There was this very beautiful woman, sitting at a table, that wouldn't dance with anyone. My buddies and several others had asked her to dance to no avail. She simply refused to dance with any of them. I said to my buddies that I bet I can get her to dance and they all laughed at me and betted money against me.

I walked over to her table and the next thing I knew we were on the floor dancing with each other. Afterwards, I walked over to my friends to high fives and the collection of my money. My one friend said what did you tell her. What did you say to her and I told him it was "top secret?"

The simple truth of the matter is that all I told her was what was actually happening? I told her that some men had betted me that she wouldn't dance with me and I know you would hate to see me lose money over a dance and she simply said, "sure would."

The secret to the dance was simply telling her the truth. I think about that sometimes and smile to myself!

Ray Jr, who is my maternal first cousin once removed. My grandmother was Luesther and she had a sister named Aunt Bessie. Aunt Bessie had a son that she named Ray Jr. He joined the Army out of Detroit and just happened to be stationed at Fort Leonard Wood at the same times as me. We decided to both take leave the base and go see our mothers one day on vacation. I had just bought a 1971 Lemans and was excited to see how it would run on the open road. As we were traveling from Ft Leonard to Detroit and then to Pontiac, he would tell me something surprising and yet predictable. He said when I left Pontiac to go live in Long Beach as a teenager that my stepdad said, "I was going to wind up in jail and that I would become nothing in life." I was shocked and actually asked John, my stepdad, and he said he never said it. He did say that "If someone tells you that you can't do something that you always do the opposite." This only made me suspect him even more that his intentions toward me were not good. I actually felt sorry for him. Here he was the only child of his mother trying to raise 6 strong willed kids and he didn't have the character to do it and so one by one he chase my mom's kids away from the house. He chased the others away, by telling them to move or locking them out of the house, but I was the one that just left. I saw the writing on the wall. I often tease my mom and tell her that she is not good at picking husband.

I later talked to Othello and he once said, "I always wondered why John treated you so bad. It was obvious that he did not like you." John even to this day talks to me like I am not there. Whenever I come to visit my mom. He always says, "Why didn't you call first?" I always tell him that "I wanted to surprise my mom." Now, my wife and I rent a motel whenever we go to Pontiac to visit my mom and to avoid any interaction between him and I. By staying at a Nice Hilton Hotel, we minimize the interactions and make the get togethers have a lot less friction and more harmony.

We invite them out to diners and restaurants and my mom jumps at the offers, but my stepdad John makes excuses for not being able to come. One time I invited both of them to breakfast at the Pancake House. around 6 am. My dad said he couldn't come because a man was coming to fix his side door. My mom said, "He is not coming until 9 am and it is 6 am" John said, "I don't want to miss him'" My mom came by herself and we had a great breakfast. He blames me for breaking up his family, but I say he got in over in over his head.

# Chapter 16

## Black Law Society at CSULB and Drury College

We started the Black Law Society at California State University Long Beach. The four of us ran into each other in our political science major classes and discovered that we all wanted to be lawyers. When I say we, I mean Jessie Hamilton was Vice President, Marshal Turner was Secretary, and Donald Hansford was the Treasurer and I being the President.

Donald Hansford, Poly High Class of 1974, has recently passed from this life to the next. He helped me co-found the Black Law Society at CSULB in 1978 along with the others. He supported me in every aspect of my life, and he was truly a brother of the highest order. He retired from the city of Long Beach and traveled the world before his passing. I rarely say this, but I love you brother, and your passing made me cry. Salud doc. Salud to a true brother...he talked the talk and walked the walk. I always thought of you as a brother even though we were not blood. You are a great man and your presence will indeed be missed. You were simply one of a kind.

We four started the Black Law Society during the Jimmy Carter

Presidency. Jimmy Carter was a peanut farmer from Georgia that defeated President Ford for the presidency. Nixon had appointed President Ford president after he resigned, and Jimmy Carter defeated the appointee Ford, primarily because Ford had pardoned Nixon. The Elephant is the symbol of the Republican and they definitely remembered that pardon on election day and elected a Democrat.

I told the Black students at CSULB that we needed to form a group to protect our interest. I argued that Black Students had been instrumental in starting the Black Studies Program at various colleges across the nation and they should have a voice in the Department. We were instrumental in having Long Beach Councilman Jim Wilson come speak to our group and in blocking the opening of Liquor stores in the primarily Afro-American 6$^{th}$ District of Long Beach.

I remember the initial meeting of the Black Law Society at CSULB and the room was so full and being overflowing with Black Students that came out of curiosity. Then the second meeting I had to ask for money for the organization. I had never asked for money from a large group of my own people in my life and to my surprise they went into their pockets and purses and started giving our organization cash.

I enjoyed being the President of the Black Law Society at CSULB. Student would sometimes ask me could they just walk with me and be seen with me on campus because I was President. We gave some of the best parties at CSULB and in 1978 we gave a party in Baldwin Hills that was simply off the chain. Women clamored for my attention like never before in my life. We each carried a gun and were ready to die for the cause in those days. I had never been in a gang as a youth and here I was in college packing a gun.

One time, three of the other officers in the Black Law Society pointed a gun at two undercover cops and we had to get an attorney to get them off. Jesse, Donald, and Marshal pulled out guns on the plainclothes Long Beach Policemen and got arrested. They were outside in front of Jesse's apartment and the police blew their horn to tell them to move out of the street so that they could pass. Words were exchanged and my Black Law Society officers pulled guns out on the cops. They were arrested immediately, and we later hired an attorney and beat the charges because the cops were in plainclothes. I would have been with them at the time and also arrested because we all carried guns at the time. I still can believe I waited until I was in college and 22 years old to start carrying a gun.

We even had a trial for a traitor in the organization because he was giving our information to our white counterpart, Law Society. We fought the Black Studies Department to change a grade of one of the officers. We meet with the famous Angela Davis and gave conferences on various Black Issues. I studied under Amen Rah and Ron Karenga was Chairman of our Black Studies Department. The latter was the one that brought Kwanzaa to the United States.

Prior to California State University Long Beach (CSULB) I went to a satellite college called Drury College out of Springfield, Missouri on the Army Base at Fort Leonard Wood. While my other soldiers and friends were getting drunk and smoking weed and partying, I went to school at night. The first class I took was Psychology101 and I was always asking questions in class. One officer in the class kept claiming it was manifest destiny for the white man to own America and it was the will of God for them to be in charge of America and that it was the will of God for the Indians to be defeated. I never debated him in class because I was a mere private and he was an officer. Many of the officers in the Army were from down south and many of the foot soldiers were from Urban areas in the 1970's and thus the classroom on base had an interesting dynamic. They would have kicked me out of the Army for insubordination if I told them how I really felt about the topic of manifest destiny being a code word for genocide and subjugation.

Drury College was the seed where I was planted and started my education and CSULB would be place where I blossomed. Drury College taught me how to look at things from a different perspective. I basically took Psychology and History classes while at Drury College. This college was headquartered in Springfield. Missouri and the instructors that taught on base were highly intelligent. Although they made few jokes and were quite serious all the time. However, Drury College helped me to become the man I am today. Drury College taught me so much and I had a year and a half of education when I left the Army and transferred those units to CSULB.

Getting back to CSULB, Beverly was my girlfriend at CSULB in those days, and she bought me a Black 's Law Dictionary as a gift on my graduation day. She was a light skinned black woman with long hair, gorgeous eyes, and a sweet smile. She was hard to seduce and yet worth every month of pursuit. She was pursued by many men in college, including a high school friend of mind named Ricky. She was gorgeous. She was sweet under the sheets and we broke up because I went over her house unannounced with my friend, Olen. She was angry that I bought another man over her house unannounced and broke up with me. I didn't understand her disgust at the time, but I definitely understand it today.

I also pursued in vain a student named Jennifer, but I never succeeded in parting the red sea of her life. She was a hard nut to crack and although I tried semester after semester, I always fell short. I bought her flowers one semester and she told everyone at school about my purchase and guys teased me relentlessly about buying flowers for a woman that wasn't my girlfriend. I replied that I thought she had died and that is why I sent flowers.

My first year of law school I took Jennifer to a Black American Law School Association Conference party and after the conference was over, everyone got up to dance, but she refused to dance with me. I asked the lady at the table adjacent to us and she gladly accepted my offer to dance. Afterwards, Jennifer would tell me it was wrong for me to bring her to the conference and dance with someone else. I said I danced with her because you would not dance with me. She and I would often go to parties together as friends, and she would get upset if I danced with someone else. I always said to her how can you get upset when we are merely friends. She was actually in love with a guy that would stand her up on dates and totally disrespected her from Los Angeles. I finally gave up the chase of her when I meant my second wife. The funny thing about life is the people who want us we usually don't want and the ones we want usually don't want us.

When I initially applied to CSULB they denied my application. My dad told me to go down to the school and ask to see the Dean of Admission. I talked to him and he said we obviously made a mistake and they admitted me to the University. I thank my dad for encouraging me to overcome the rejection and some lessons that he taught me would really help me later in life.

In high school, my teacher, Dee Andrews, introduced us, as a class, to a speaker and professor named Sleepy Montgomery also known as Amen Rah. Later in life, I would attend CSULB and take Amen Rah's classes and this same professor would allow me to speak at his conferences and even invite me to speak in front of his classes after I graduated and went to law school.

I am where I am today because great men and women have spoken into my life. I am a teacher today because teachers spoke into my life. None of us make it on our own and we owe our various successes to the many people that spoke into our lives and for these men and women I am eternally grateful.

At CSULB, a Mexican girl named Cecilia said we can mess around, but my dad does not like Blacks. She said I could meet her at the corner around her house and she would climb out the window and meet me around the corner. I passed on the opportunity. I really like the girl, but I simply didn't want to take the risk. I really did not want her to be climbing out her window as an adult and my climbing into someone's house like I climbed into the women's barracks while in the Army days were simply over. She was a beautiful woman I regret that we never consummated the relationship.

I was also working at night in a nursing home while attending college at this time. This Black lady was my co-worker and having sex with a white man that was her boss at work late at night. Every morning her husband would come pick her up with their kids in the car. She would kiss her husband and kids when they came to pick her up. I would just say he wouldn't believe me if I told him, so I kept my mouth shut. That is why I say all Black women were not raped in slavery, a few of them were happy to sleep with the slave masters and some were willing participants as was evidenced by this sistah.

I mostly partied with Marshal and Jesse during my college days. We often drove from Long Beach to Los Angeles and sat in Jessie garage and talked about life. Jesse told us that when he was in a gang that he would shoot up party for fun. One day I had to convince him not to kill a brother that had stepped on his shoe at a party. Jesse said he was going to go to his car and get a gun and shoot him. I told him please do not shoot him and offered to dust off his shoes.

Jesse said no he has to die. I think Jesse was angry that his dad had left him as a child and so he was angry at the slightest insult and his anger was often scapegoated to the wrong people. Somehow, I talked him out of not shooting the guy and we all left the party. I wonder does that Black guy knows how close he came to death

My Uncle Robert Tyson came with my sister Ramona to my graduation from CSULB and so did my Uncles Obie and Dwight. Ramona said you said it and did it and my Aunt Ulato aka Turk give me a check for $25 as a gift. I do not remember what the commencement speaker said at graduation, but I do remember my mom and stepdad did not show up and my sister said you said it and you did it. I will never forget those words. You said it and you did it. I also couldn't believe my Aunt gave me the $25. To a hungry college student $25 was like a million dollars in 1978.

Later in life I would learn that the power of life and death is in the tongue, but at that time, I didn't know those words, and yet the spoken seed came to fruition on that day.

Look in the mirror today, you mighty men and women of God, salute yourself, and say," I said it and I did it!" Enjoy your next journey and get ready for your new destination! Nothing beats setting a goal and achieving it in life.

I dated Jessica in my senior years at CSULB. She was tall and fine. We went to the movies on our first date. While we were waiting for the movie to start. She told me the story of three rats in a box. She said there were three rats trapped in a box. Two of the rats were males and one was female. She said the female rat was tired of being in the trapped box and asked one of the male rats, how do I get out. The male rat said if you go to bed with me then I will tell you how to get out. She went to bed with him and then said tell me how to get out of this box and the male rat replied If I knew how to get out of this box, I would of left a long time ago. She then goes and ask the second male rat will he help her get out of the box and he replies only if you go the bed with me. She goes to bed with him and he gives her the same reply that if I knew how to get out of here, I would have been out a long time ago. She got so mad and angry that she got out of the box. Then Jessica asked me. "Do you want to know how she got out of the box." I said, "Yes." She replied,} I will tell you if you go to bed with me". I laughed so hard and left the theater right then and there. I had never heard a story like hers. and I couldn't wait until the movie was over to be with her. I didn't even ask the theater for my money back. I just left.

The last girl I dated while at CSULB was Margaret from Westminster. She was a high-class Jamaican, erudite, and a sharp dresser. She was saving herself for marriage and I respected that fact. We did a lot of things together, but she never surrendered her virginity. I am sure she is very successful in life. Her dad and mom were pushing her to excel. She was one of the kindest people that I meant in my life. I introduced her cousin to my friend, Olen, and he, true to form. dogged her cousin out.

One day while in college, I knocked on Robbie's door and he would not let me in the house, Leo, my classmate was also beating on the door. Robbie was with Leo's girlfriend at the time and Robbie was afraid Leo was going to beat him up. I said open the door. I knocked on the door and said Robbie, it is Hudena, let me in. He refused. He lived upstairs in a second story apartment. I recklessly climbed a pole to the top of the roof of his apartment and walked on the roof to the back door of his apartment and came down and opened up his back door. He was surprised. I told him to open the door and let Leo in the room. I told him Leo would not mess with him. I opened the front door and let Leo in and told him to take his woman and go. He took his woman and left. Robbie thank me and yet later on in life Leo would die prematurely and Robbie would hit on my wife.

As I recall my own graduation from CSULB; I was so excited about the day and thought for sure a band should be playing or maybe even a parade because I was graduating, but I soon realize the joy is actually found in the journey and the destination is simply the icing on the cake. I can still recall hugging my friends that had accomplished the same feat. The cap and gown man collecting the items after the graduation but isolating me and telling me that I could keep my cap - while collecting all the others. I guess I was bubbling over with joy on that day. It was a phenomenal triumph over struggles, distractions, and setbacks that made that day so special. A high school classmate Bill had quit college because his dad had died, and I told him that I would never quit college if my dad died and yet a year later my dad died in 1977. After he died, I wanted to quit but didn't because of what I had told Bill. I stayed focused and graduated in 1978. I was elated.

# Chapter 17

## LAW SCHOOL

President Reagan is President as of 1980 and he is implementing a Conservative Agenda across America. The streets are becoming populated with homeless people and I just finished reading a book by Karl A. Lamb called "As Oranges Goes" and he talked about the future of technology and how many technocrat superfluous people would be useless in a technological world because they didn't have technological skills. In the ensuing years, I would watch as technology increases and simultaneously did the homeless population in America. Karl Lamb had prophesized it long before it happened.

The Bar Exam in California was given in three days and if you didn't pass, you could retake the days that you scored poorly on the Exam. They suddenly changed the rules and if you missed a portion of the exam then you had to take all three days over again. The State Bar rule change would have a devastating effect on many law school students, those that those that didn't pass the Bar initially were told they could no longer just take the portion they missed but they must take the entire three day exam over if they failed any portion of it. In short, new examinees had to take all three days of the bar exam over and over again if they did not pass. I read that it was done to keep lawyers from flooding the marketplace. However, many law students would never pass the bar due to this new policy and I was one of them.

I was an Epicurean in Law school. An Epicurean is a disciple or student of the Greek philosopher Epicurus. The Epicureans were devoted to sensual enjoyment, especially that derived from fine food and drink. In other words, the whore in me came out in Law School. I was screwing everything that moved at Western State University from students to teachers to administrators.

I started law school at Western State College of Law and finished up at American College of Law. I would meet my wife in the second year of law school, and we married in my third year. Western State University is where I meet my wife and also meet my Waterloo or Rubicon when I was academically dismissed from Law School for poor grades. I would go and enroll at American College of law and finish my last year of law school there.

On the positive side, law school taught me a new way of thinking and a new way of looking at life. They taught us that life was not simply Black and White but rather if was Gray and right and wrong depended on the ability to persuade others to your point of view. It was often said Liberals became Conservatives after attending law school and vice versa. They also taught you to look at arguments from your opponent 's perspective to defeat his arguments.

The first year I caught an ulcer in my stomach because the studying was so difficult. It was the most homework I had ever done in my life. Law School made college look like Kindergarten. We had to read voluminous case and then brief them and pull out the relevant points and dismiss the superfluous matters.

I remember I was nearly financial broke every time I went to law class. I can remember begging my parent to send me money for law school to no avail. My dad Robert was now deceased, and my stepdad and mom said they just didn't have the money and could not help me. My stepmom Gloria had left for Alexandria, Louisiana and didn't provide any help. I remember staring at people as they ate in their lunch in the lunchroom at law school. My mouth watering and my stomach growling as I watch them eat delicious food.

One day when I hung up the telephone, after begging my mom for money, a bunch of change came out of the phone booth. I rationalize that it was gift from God to help me out of my distress. I remember using the money to buy me a coke, fries, and a hamburger. I then caught the bus from Long Beach to Fullerton to go to law school. As I set on a bus bench in Orange County to catch the bus on the final leg to law school, a white guy, on the passenger side of the car, came along and called me a Nigger. I threw the coke at his passing car, the French fries, and the burger. As he sped away, I watched all those cars driving over my food while my stomach was still aching. It taught me a valuable lesson, however, and that was never let your emotions overrule your logic. I remember my stepdad's words of apply the stimulus and get the response and that white boy had applied the stimulus and got the response he expected. I had loss the very food needed to satisfy my hunger. I vowed that day forward to never again let a white man or any other man apply the stimulus and get their response.

I dated my co-worker in law school. She was my co-worker at the VA office. Since I was an Army Vet, they hired me to talk to Veterans and help them to obtain benefits form the VA. I also worked part-time at the VA Hospital as Phlebotomist drawing blood from patients.

I pursued my co-worker zealously and one day and she finally agreed to go out with me. We went to the Quiet Cannon in Long Beach and I tried to no avail to seduce her. She claims she was my boss and simply could not mess with the help and I claimed we only had an employment relationship from 12 to 4 each day and after that time we were non co-workers. She laughed. She never did give into any of my desires until my second year when I meet my wife. She then pursued me, but by that time I was no longer interested in her. It is funny but sometimes when a fine woman becomes interested in you that people who hardly notice you will all of a sudden become interested in you as well. My coworker Dianne in law school did not become interested in me until I met my future wife Jackie. When Jackie stepped into my life, everyone was giving me play. By the way, Dianne was white, and Jackie was black.

I also like this coworker white girl named Candice while I was in law school. I kept hitting on her and she would laugh at my jokes and compliments me, but not give me the time of day. She would just laugh and walk away. I would say do you like Baby Ruth Candy Bars and she would say no, and I would say well, they are big, chocolate, and full of nuts and she would smile and walk away, Today, those words would be a case of sexual harassment but in those days it was not.

Then one day, out of nowhere, Candice, called me, while I was sitting at my desk. She said I need to see you. I cannot stop thinking about you. I was really shocked because I thought my words were simply falling on deaf ears. We meet after work and kissed and stuff and grinded, but we never did have sex.

She said she wanted to have sex but cringed at every motel I went to that day. She said, "That is not the one." She told me she once had sex with a doctor, and that he had took her to the Hilton Hotel. I told her that I did not have Hilton Hotel money because I was in law school. We never did have sex. She was extremely high class and really like men with money. Money that I simply did not have at the time. We meet a few more times for kissing and hugging but we never made love, she even wrote me love letters, but she never made love to me. I think she was curious about a black man but her for desire for wealth and status were more overpowering.

Also, I messed with a gorgeous Ebony woman named Sandra in Long Beach. She was fine and mostly dated white guys. She was rich and bourgeoise and we became sexually involved. She was the prominent daughter of a doctor in Long Beach. She was an aspiring actress and I meant her at a play in Long Beach. Her co actor told me he was playing Dr King in the play but that I was the real Dr King, I thought that was high praise to a young man that wanted to be lawyer. I convinced Sandra to give me her entire check from work. Guys had always told me that I had the gift of Gab but I never realize it until I asked for money from the Black Law Society one day and then also when I convinced this woman to give me her entire paycheck from work.

I also messed with a Central American named Sophia in Law School. I like having sex with her because her eyes would roll back inside her head like a slot machine when she would come. I believe some man or woman got the idea for the slot machine from the having sex with their mate. I have never had another woman eye roll inside their head while making love and that is why she stands out in my life. I was in shock the first time I saw it.

Also, when she would engage in fellatio, she would come in her panties. She was the freakiest woman I would ever meet in my life. Sometimes when she was having fellatio with me, she would be bent over in the bed giving me head and I would hear splatter against the wall. I realize now that her come was hitting the wall. I would say to her did you hear that noise and she would always say no. She like oral sex more than regular sex. I think because she was so religious that regular sex was considered prohibitive, so she started out early in life doing oral sex in lieu of regular sex.

I think in her mind, regular sex was taboo but oral sex was okay. She would often swallow me and ask for more. We eventually broke up and she married another guy. I wished them well. She invited me to the wedding, but I did not go.

I also messed with another white girl named Kathryn, Kathryn also loved oral sex more than regular sex. She told me her uncle had messed with her as a little kid. She would often wait until I was in the tub taking a bath and come into the bathroom and get me off while I was in the tub. She took oral sex to another level and would hum while giving head. When we did make love, she would come so much that the entire bed got wet.

Last but not least, Barbara was the other one, she was Mexican, and she was the first woman to let me have sex in the front and the back. She would say I found a Frog in my panty draw as her signal to have sex.

She was good at oral sex, but she could win the Olympic for doggie style love making. She had this backward 69 position that I had never seen in my life. She would sit on top of you while you were laying down and then turn around toward your feet and ride you like a horse. She was a good lover, but she did not like oral sex as much as my previous girlfriends.

While I was whoring around in law school and messing with different women, I was also protesting against injustices. While in law school, I always found time to protest some injustices. I marched in the Ron Settles case. He was the young CSULB student and outstanding football athlete that was murdered by the Signal Hill Police. He was found hung in his jail cell. We marched to protest his brutal killing in a jail cell. Amen Rah and many others were in the March to protest this injustice. Eventually the City of Signal Hill settled the case with the Attorney John Cochran but police abuse against African American continues to this day.

I don't think anyone will ever forget Ron Settles. He had so much promise and potential and hatred killed him in one moment. The police claimed he committed suicide, but he was severely beaten by officer on June 2, 1981.

I marched in the parade with my teacher Amen Rah and countless others to protest the killing and eventually the family settled the case for a million dollars with Johnny Cochran as the lead attorney.

I also helped my friend Steve win the nomination for President of BALSA which is Black American Law School Association and then the next year I ran for the Presidency and loss by a close vote of 12 to 11.

# Chapter 18

## Paralegal and Politics

When I initially started working in the legal field, I worked for an attorney named Stanley Best, III. He had a rather prosperous law firm in Inglewood, Calif, back in the days. He told me that he would give me a job if I could serve this gangster divorce papers. Serving the gangster in Inglewood was dangerous. He told me he would shoot me if I gave him the papers. I told him it was my duty. I dropped the papers by his shoes and walked away. I kept waiting to hear bullets, but he never shot me.

Another time Attorney Best had me serve the Head of Hughes Aircraft divorce papers. I went to Hughes Aircraft and told the front clerk that the Head of Security was my best friend and I wanted to surprise him with a visit. She called him up and he came down and I serve him with the divorce papers. He got on his walkie talkie and told them not to let me off the premises. I started running to my car and drove off quickly before they could catch me. He was a black guy and he was leaving his wife for a white girl. However, by the time I got back to the office. They had reconciled their marriage and dropped the divorce.

In the same office as Attorney Best was an insurance firm in which the secretary therein was the daughter of the owner of the insurance firm. I got into a conversation with her one day and she was a white girl and she is bragging on how much she loved her black boyfriend and that occasionally he would give her a "golden shower". This term piqued my interest and I asked her what exactly was a "golden shower" and she explained to me that it is when someone urinate all over your body during or after sex. I was appalled and shocked at her response. Her boyfriend had convinced her that urinating all over her body was in his words a" golden shower" and thus a reward in her mind.

If you have ever heard me teach. I often quote these words, "Don't let people urinate on you and then tell you that it is just rain." Well, that particular quote comes from this particular conversation many years ago with her.

Fast forward to today, in my opinion that is exactly what Donald Trump is doing, he is urinating on the masses and trying to convince them that it is a "golden shower". He is suddenly a friend of the oppressed, the downtrodden, the rejected, and even minorities. The very people he has urinated on for countless years. He wants us to believe that the Fox cares about the chickens. He will obviously fool some of us, but he will never fool the bulk of us because there is quite a difference between water and piss and no one should ever piss on us and tell us that it is rain from heaven because the bulk of us actually know the difference and we will simply not be fooled. Don't you be fooled.

My paralegal days were in the 1980 during the Presidency of Ronald Reagan. He and his conservative Agenda is sweeping the country. In America, the pendulum often swings back between Liberal and Conservative and in the 1980's it swung toward the Conservative Agenda. Funds were cut for any programs that helped the black and poor and Conservatives rejoicing in their victory. His presidency will soon be followed by a more moderate President Bush. I would later write a letter to President Bush when I had problem obtaining a VA Loan to buy a house. He would respond with a letter and shortly thereafter my VA Loan would be approved, and I got my first house.

My first client, after law school, was my maternal grandmother Luesther. Someone stole about $10,000 out of her checking account and I got the money put back in her account at Bank of America and she gave me a $100 for my effort. An underpayment but then again, she was my grandmother. Apparently, her son and my uncle were stealing from her. Her son and my uncle would never speak to me again after I recovered the money and exposed their deception.

My Uncle Dwight hired me to work for him right after law school. He was a doctor and a lawyer, and he hired me as his legal assistant. He was of counsel to a law firm called Grant and Duncan in Los Angeles. Donna was an attorney in the firm. She was one of the smartest attorneys I ever met in my life. She would teach me how to write briefs and do legal research. At some point in our friendship she and I started having sex back in the days.

We often did drugs and sex together. However, she kept doing drugs after I quit and later become psychotic from drug use. She was later disbarred because of her abuse of cocaine. She was married and one day she went home and confessed to her husband that she had being seeing me. My wife came to me one morning in the shower and said some man is on the phone claiming you are sleeping with his wife. I answered the phone and told him to never call this house again as long as he lives, and he never did. I left her because the relationship had come too close to home and she later started messing with a partner in the law firm. She and the partner would get high on coke in the middle of the day in the office and later on I would leave the firm.

I stopped working for my Uncle Dwight because he had stated gambling and paychecks became erratic. He claimed the Russian bosses did not pay their employees and they remain loyal and I guess he was trying to see if it would work with me. I, however, would go see his clients and collect their money and used that money as my paycheck to feed my family and myself. One day he found out I was collecting the money and he let me go. While the Russian Mafia had waited months without pay, I was not willing to wait a week without a paycheck. We did not talk for several years after that fact and he never invited me to his wedding to his second wife Yolanda.

I built up a nice clientele doing paralegal work on my own during this time. I meet interesting people and helped a lot of people that were facing various legal dilemmas

I was even fined $500 by a Judge and took the case on appeal and won. I did my own appeal and was so happy when I won the appeal.

One time I was standing in line at the bankruptcy court to file some paperwork for a client. The clerk motions me forward to take my papers. As the female clerk is talking to me and examining my papers, this elderly white man, obviously thinking I am invisible, walks up to the female clerk, ignoring everyone in line, and started asking her repeated questions, as if I am not even there!

The female clerk replies," I am helping this gentleman right now, I will be with you shortly. The elderly white man looks at me real hard. I said to him and the clerk, "Well you know white men don't have any respect for black men." The elderly white man says immediately, "Well, I was here first." I, in reply, said, "The Indians were here first." The clerk busted out laughing, and the white male just stared at me and got back in line. I said to them both, you know I was just teasing, but was I?

My son went to rent a building in Riverside for an upcoming function and he called me to tell me that the manager of the bldg.

said," I know your father, he helped me with a legal matter many years ago" and so she gave him a substantial discount on renting the building! His phone call really warmed my heart. The good or bad that you do for others in life can often come back to bless or hurt your very own family. I love cyclical good!!

I worked for Attorney Best in Inglewood. He was a very smart attorney, but someone got him hooked on cocaine. I came to work one day, and the other employees said Attorney Best is not paying us today. I wondered to myself, what is it with these Black Attorneys not paying their employees. I told my co-workers that he is going to pay me today. I rushed into his closed-door office and he was snorting cocaine and I demanded he pay me a check right now. I defied his orders not to let anyone in his office. He thought I had loss my mind. He wrote me a check and I cashed it and it that same day. I was so mild mannered that he was shocked to see my alter ego. He called my wife and asked was everything okay at my house and was I at home. He was scared to go to his own office for fear that I might come back to the office. However, what I noticed was none of those other employees had the nerve to ask for their check. I was the only one that demanded payment.

On another occasion, Attorney Best took me to lunch one time, and I billed him for the lunch hour, and he said how can you bill me for the lunch hour when I bought you lunch. I said because the lunch was on your time. I was not free to go where I wanted to eat for that entire hour and so that is a billable hour and he conceded to my point of view.

I also worked for Attorney Johnson in Pasadena. He was a brilliant attorney. One time a lady once came to our office because she was involved in a car accident. The Insurance company was going to pay the lease car company for damages to the car and not pay the lessee a penny. My attorney said there was nothing he could do about that matter. He was just going to handle the personal injury portion of her case. I wrote a lady to the lease company without my attorney's knowledge and told them it was unfair for them to keep that money and that it violated the implied covenant of good faith and fair dealings inherent in all contracts in California. They subsequently paid her the $10, 000 and yet she told me she had not heard anything from the Insurance Company. I realized that she had ripped me off and I told the attorney what I had done, and he took one third of her recovery. In short, she paid $3,333 to my boss instead of $100 to me. All she had to do was pay me a $100 but she wound up paying thousands because of her greed. It taught me that people are greedy when it comes to money. The Attorney took 1/3 of her money from her settlement and he didn't fire me.

I always wanted to sleep with an Asian woman. In Jr High school, the black guys always said they had horizontal vaginas instead of vertical ones. This curiosity got my attention, but I would never be able to fill that desire even though I realize now that the motivation was based on a falsehood. All women 's vaginas are basically the same. However, I did get close to consummating the desire once. I had a paralegal and tax business and one of my clients lived in Seal Beach. I went over her house to do her taxes. After her taxes were done. She essentially told me that she amorously wanted me. I at the time was married and preaching at the same time and I told her it was not right to commit adultery. I explained to her that adultery was a sin and that God frowned on fornication.

After I left her house, I said who was that guy? What in the hell is wrong with you? I realize now that was the new me and I was not going to be unfaithful. The temptation was obviously there but my convictions kept me strong. She never again called me to do her Taxes, so in a way I won and loss.

I ran for political office twice in Long Beach. Once in 1984 and again in 1986. I ran in the 4th District which was predominantly white and again in the 6th District, after the sudden death of Council man Jim Wilson which was predominantly Afro American. I loss both races. I would learn later that my former high school teacher Dee Andrew would run for the 6th District office and win. He too had a bout with drug addiction but recovered and became a success in life, He is further proof that we should never give up on ourselves.

I received a ticket for being parked for more than 2 hours at the law library in Riverside at 11:07 am in the month of April. I argued to the City that I was in Moreno Valley at 9:15 on a phone call that particular day and my phone records could attest to my location.

I also argued that Moreno Valley is 14 miles from Riverside and that it would take me at least 23 minutes to get to the Riverside Law Library. In short, the earliest that I could of practically arrived in Riverside was 9:38 a.m., and therefore 2 hours of parking would be 11:38a.m., and since I received the ticket at 11:07a.m., that someone had wrote the ticket prematurely and made a serious error.

I got a letter in the mail today stating the ticket had been dismissed.

I love standing up for my rights and the rights of others. God is so good!!

I am in an awfully long line at the San Bernardino IRS office today. At least a block long or longer. I have been in line for approximately an hour. Abruptly, this lady comes out of nowhere and cuts in front of me. I said, "Excuse me ma' am, but where you here before and you just came back? "

She says, "Yes I was."

The two ladies in front of me and her say, "No she wasn't."

I said, "Ma'am you can't cut in front of me, but you can cut behind me."

This tattooed brother says, and I will quote him verbatim, "This nigger is crazy telling the lady she can cut in front of me. Nigger, is you crazy telling the lady she can cut in front of me? This crazy assed nigger has loss his mind." He is shouting in a loud voice and ranting at me.

I said, "Very calmly, if you don't want her in front of you, then send her to the end of the line. "

He starts to prance and dance as if he is going to do something to me while still ranting and raving.

The lady in front of us, a different lady, tells the woman that cut in line, "You are up there", indicating she is closer to the front and that she shouldn't have cut in front of me. The lady that cut in line finally sees her husband and realizes that she cut the wrong place in line and returns to her man up front.

In the meantime, this black guy is still prancing and talking to himself and ranting about me being a crazy assed nigger. Obviously trying to provoke me to fight him.

I am calm outside, but angry inside, that this minor incident has escalated to this point. I know, as all people that the slightest thing can get you killed when you are dealing with your own in the ghettos of life in America. I believe a flying Eagle should never fight a barking dog, but this guy is making it hard.

He looks hard at me and I look hard at him. Of course, I am always locked and loaded.

Out of nowhere, his 9 or 10-year-old daughter runs up to him in the line and says, "Daddy, can I have the keys to the car? "He gives her the keys and his daughter run the keys to her mom, that is sitting in a Van watching this drama play out, when finally, he calms down.

(Everyone knows you can die in the ghettoes of life for simply stepping on a person's shoes.)

I am finally out of the line and escorted into the IRS office.

I got into the IRS office first and then he and his pregnant wife or girlfriend and daughter, who has subsequently joined him in line, came into the office next. The two of them are sitting in one chair, her on his lap. The IRS security guard comes to me and says, "Can I ask you move to over one seat so the two of them may have separate chairs." I said, "No problem." I then reach out my hand and said I see we meet again. I am Hudena and he tells me his name and we both sit quietly next to each other, most likely thinking about what almost happened.

Another day in the ghetto of life!

One time in Long Beach I went to this club on Anaheim Blvd. I think it was called Cecil's Palace, but I am not quite sure anymore, and I met this voluptuous looking young lady and she told me that she was single and had her own place and so after a few drinks and dances we left the club and walked to her apartment a few blocks away.

Afterwards, we were sitting on her couch kissing and suddenly someone started knocking on the door rather harshly. She went to the door's peephole and came back in a panic and said, "That is my boyfriend and you have to go out the back window before he sees you. "

I said, "You told me you didn't have a boyfriend."

She said, "We broke up and I think he wants to get back together."

I said, "I do not climb out back windows, so you need to keep him out."

She said, I have to let him in." I then, with my stupid self, said, "Let him in because I am not climbing out any back window. The way I walk in is always the way I walk out"

The young lady abruptly let him in and he just looked at me real hard and I looked at him real hard - like - is there a problem!

He then went and got on the phone, because they didn't have

cell phones in those days, and asked some of his friends to come over to the apartment to help him remove me. On that note, I walked out of the front door of the apartment.

I am sitting here thinking that in my 20's I had more testosterone than brains and I cannot believe I did those things in those days.

I should have hit that back window rather quickly but those were the days and that was the audacious me!

Always remember that we have two minds and the "critical mind" will always discourage you while the "creative mind" will encourage you.

The critical mind exists to create doubt and discouragement, but you - like I, will not listen to him or her. :))))

May all your dreams come true and remember your best days are always in front of you but stop listening to the critical and discouraging mind!

Do not be offended but is not it interesting that a Black gangbanger writes on a physical wall that this is his territory.

A Mexican gangbanger posted on a physical wall that this is his territory.

An Asian gangbanger posted on a physical wall that this is his territory.

Meanwhile, this Jewish guy, that does not belong to any gang, goes to Harvard, and subsequently says that anyone can post on my internet wall called "FB" and he subsequently becomes a billionaire.

In the meantime, the Black guy, Mexican guy, and Asian guy, are all in jail and yet they came up with idea of posting on a wall.

Life is just so unfair

His neighbor, Barbara McCoy, also took a liking to me and gave me sage advice about the streets. She offered her house up for bail and all the criminals in Long Beach came to her to use her house as collateral for bail. Her son had robbed banks and was involved with the Crips. She knew everyone and introduced me to so many clients. Some I would help and others I would refer to lawyers.

I went to this club in Carson to watch Ali fight. As we were waiting for the fight to come on, this guy went and stood in front of the television. No one said anything to him. I shouted from my seat, "Hey man, move so we can watch the fight" He didn't say anything. He just turned around looked at me real hard and walked outside the club. I grabbed my wife and said let's go. We will see Ali fight another time. The fact that he didn't say anything was notice to me that he intended to go get something. Whenever he came back, I was not there. My insights into human behavior and knowing when to hold, fold, and run has kept me alive this long in life. Some people simply don't read signals.

I love, defending my own cases and prosecuting my own cases. I sued a bank for racial discrimination. They refused to cash a check for my daughter and refused to open an account for me. I sued them pursuant to the 42 USC 1981 and the trial court dismissed the lawsuit because they said while it was possible that I was discriminated that it was not plausible, and the Bank simply made a mistake. I appealed to the 9$^{th}$ circuit Court of Appeal and won. The 9th Circuit Court of Appeal said I did indeed have a plausible cause of action and ordered the case remanded back to the trial court. I was overjoyed with excitement. I had appealed and won, and I was not an attorney. The Appellate Court said that I had presented a plausible cause of action for violation of the 1964 Civil Rights Act and Unruh Civil Rights Act against the bank. I was so proud of myself because I wasn't a lawyer and yet I defended my own case on the Appellate level. Another time a Federal Bankruptcy Judge fined me $500 for practicing law without a license in preparing a Bankruptcy Petition. I took the case to the Bankruptcy Appellate Court and they reversed the decision and said I did not have to pay the $500 because I was denied the right to cross examine my accuser.

I love defending and fighting my own legal actions and know I would have been a great lawyer if I had of passed the bar. I am able to make creditors reversed late fees simply by writing a letter under the implied covenant of good faith and fair dealing that is inherent in all contracts in California. The other day I settled a case against my dentist for negligently performing dental work.

I sued a bank in Alta Loma, California for illegal racial discrimination and disparate treatment. They told my daughter and I that we had to live within a 5 to 6-mile radius of the bank to open a bank account. Has anyone ever told you that you have to live within a 5 to 6-mile radius of the bank in order to open a bank account? We had proper identification and good credit and the check was drawn on an attorney that had a trust bank account at their bank and they still wouldn't cash the check or open up an account for either of us?

One of the best decisions that I ever made in life was to go to law school. It actually taught me a new way of thinking. I have used the law to sue for houses, cars, and also sued medical facilities, the veteran administration, mortgage lenders, construction companies, and even insurance companies, and a host of other institutions that are simply too numerous to name. I do not believe in letting people run over me. My credit card company fined me $25 dollars for a late fee. I wrote them a letter and they reverse the fee.

I once sued a company for repossessing my Aries car and I actually got it back along with money for them taking my car. It is still one of the best decisions I have ever made in my life even though I am not a lawyer!

# Chapter 19

## DRUGS

I have never told anyone this before but when I was 18 years old, back in 1972, I was arrested for possession of Marijuana. The police pulled a friend and I over in Long Beach, California and put me under arrest because the weed fell out of my glove compartment when he asked for my registration.

I spent three days in jail and finally went to see the Judge. He told me that it was good I had joined the Army, several months before, and that because I had joined the Army, he would drop all the charges against me and also seal my record.

The Judge showed me some mercy. He granted me a pass in life.

The law cannot always be rigid. It must be flexible and fair and show mercy. I never again got in trouble with the law for weed and I think that Judge for seeing something in me that day that even I did not see at the time.

I was a terrible drug addict and even wrote my mom a bounced check during this period of my life.

I even remember trying to score on Christmas and knowing it was also my mom's and sister LaSharron birthdays, I still pursued the score and it did not stop knocking on doors until I scored some drugs. One side of me said you are drowning in the abyss of life and the other sign of me said you are flying high. I was obviously conflicted and out of control. One side of me said stop and the other side of me said score and I kept going until I scored.

One day my drug journey took me to meet a guy that was a Heroin addict in Carson, California. I couldn't believe he was a Heroin addict because he owed a nice house and went to work every day. He told me he had been on the stuff for nine years and he told me to stop messing with cocaine or it would destroy me. I would not heed his warnings and kept smoking cocaine. I would often bust the glass pipe I used to smoke it and then make a pipe out of aluminum foil. I was indeed loss. One time, someone put speed in the cocaine and my heart sped up so fast that I thought I was dying. I told my wife, who never did drugs, that I think I am dying because my heart is racing rapidly. My wife called the fire department and they came to my house and told me I was okay, but my heart was racing. They said someone had pit speed in my cocaine. They left my residence and treated me and told me my heart was racing but that I was okay.

I still did not stop messing with drugs. The guy that sold me the drugs asked to go with me to see me smoke it and I said No. He obviously knew it was laced with speed.

Drugs often start off as a monkey on your back They are initially fun and exciting to play around with in life, but they soon turn into a Gorilla on your back.

I started out smoking Marijuana at about 16 years old as a junior in High School at Long Beach Poly. I never bought it, but I would smoke it if a friend or relative had it. I later came out of the Army and stopped smoking it for years while attending law school but after law school I would take it up again and then graduate to smoking Cocaine and even Heroin.

Today, friends on the golf course smoke Marijuana and often

ask do I want a hit and I always refuse. They asked me why and I tell them Marijuana was the pathway drug that led me to Cocaine and Heroin and they always laugh, but I remain steadfast in my refusal to engage in smoking any type of dope. People chide me with reasoning such as God made it and I always reply God also made Poison Ivy.

(By the way, many people won't tell you this fact, but the "gateway" to many of these drugs and the common denominator is often "weed" formally known as Marijuana)

I have tried my best to warn my kids and grandkids against the evil of drugs. I hope they heed my advice.

I think the Black men and women of the future will be mostly nerds. They will be very smart and technologically savvy and very computer literate. They will be upwardly mobile and pragmatists. They will treat their opposite gender women with the utmost respect and raise even sharper kids.

The gangsters of today will mostly be dead or in jail and what will actually emerge and survive in the future will be an intelligentsia of nerds and they will simply not kill their own people but will value and treasure them and actually build up their communities and drugs will be taboo.

They will stay away from drugs and destruction and actually focus on education and upward status and then as W. E. B. Dubois once said, "the talented tenth will lead us all to the promised land" envisioned by Dr. King.....I won't be here on that day but let me know if my vision is correct.

In my lifetime I have seen people smoke "scherm" (elephant tranquilizer) take acid, smoke, and also sniff coke (cocaine), take "meth" and even shoot heroin. These drugs are put in our community to actually exploit us and take our money and then oppress us and keep us down and away from our God-given destiny. The purpose is to hinder our upward mobility.

Don't let drugs, legal and illegal, hold you back from receiving what God has actually planned for your life. The devil, enemy, opposition, whatever you want to call him or her, wants to actually destroy your life; but God wants you to live an abundant, quality, and prosperous life.

I was a mess when I got into smoking cocaine. I would bust the pipe and tell myself I am not doing this anymore and the next week make a pipe out of aluminum foil. I would make $600 dollars and say I only going to spend $200 on Cocaine and take the other $400 to the wife and I would often come home broke. I was a mess.

One time in Long Beach while I was messing with drugs, I went to this club on Anaheim Blvd. I think it was called Cecil's Palace, but I am not quite sure anymore, and I met this voluptuous looking young lady and she told me that she was single and had her own place and so after a few drinks and dances we left the club and walked to her apartment a few blocks away.

Afterwards, we were sitting on her couch kissing and suddenly someone started knocking on the door rather harshly. She went to the door's peephole and came back in a panic and said, "That is my boyfriend and you have to go out the back window before he sees you. "

I said, "You told me you didn't have a boyfriend."

She said, "We broke up and I think he wants to get back together."

I said, "I do not climb out back windows, so you need to keep him out."

She said, "I have to let him in." I then, with my stupid self, said, "Let him in because I am not climbing out any back window. The way I walk in is always the way I walk out"

The young lady abruptly let him in and he just looked at me real hard and I looked at him real hard - like - is there a problem!

He then went and got on the phone, because they didn't have cell phones in those days, and asked some of his friends to come over to the apartment to help him remove me.

On that note, I walked out of the front door of the apartment.

I am sitting here thinking that in my 20's I had more testosterone than brains and I cannot believe I did those things in those days. I should have hit that back window rather quickly but those were the days and that was the audacious me!

I also remember going to buy some chicken at Church's. I looked behind me and saw two black men rushing toward me. I perceived mischief and I turned around and said could one of you brothers give me a dime to pay for this chicken because I do not have enough money. They looked at each other and then looked at me and one reached in his pocket and gave me a dime and then they both walked away. I always say that I robbed the robbers. I have always been good at reading nonverbal cues and that art has prolonged my life.

Stay away from drugs. They are a scourge to our community and to our society. Ask for help or counseling or assistance immediately if not sooner.

You can live a drug free life. You can come out of the negative into the marvelous positive light of being drug free.

Drugs start off as a monkey on your back because they are fun and exciting, but they soon turn into a gorilla on your back and a nightmare in your life and the lives of others.

Do not be popular, instead be right!!

One time the LAPD pulled me over in Los Angeles. My wife was following me. She did not mess with drugs, but I did. When they pulled me over because they had witnessed me leave a drug house in Los Angeles. My wife jumped out of the car and started yelling at the two carloads of cops that had pulled me over. She screamed that they did not have probable cause and that her dad was a cop and the pulling me over was harassment. One of the cops said to me, "Can you please calm her down." I told my wife, "Take the money I had gave you to the bank and that I would handle this situation." The cop thanked me for calming my wife down and soon thereafter they let me go. My wife and I laugh at it now, but she was very irate at the moment.

Another time my wife came home and saw me getting high on cocaine with my friend, Ronnie. She ran in the bedroom and grabbed our gun and pointed it at Ronnie and I. Ronnie ran out the house and wrecked his car getting away. I kept smoking the cocaine and told my wife," Let me take one more hit before you shoot me" She knew I was gone out of my mind and put the gun away.

One night I had a dream that I was going to purchase some cocaine and this guy was going to stab me in the back and take my money. The dream was so real that I woke up in the middle of the night sweating. My wife suggested I go to a Cocaine Anonymous Meeting and I heeded her advice.

I finally went to a meeting for people on cocaine and the speaker said some of us are putting money into pockets with holes in them. I said that is me. I prided myself on the ability to make money, but I was a fool at saving it because I was giving it all to the drug dealer. The speaker went on to tell us that drug addicts had vivid imagination because they came up with new ideas every day on how to get drugs. He said some of us should be CEO of Fortune 500 companies. I added up what I made in a day and then what I made in a month and then what I made in a year and I never messed with drugs again. I moved away from Long Beach to Riverside and never looked back. I liked drugs but I liked money more. I now spend my money on me, my wife, and kids and give to charities and political elections and play Golf. I am so much happier.

I am glad I left drugs behind me. I am happy to save money these days. Drive nice cars, travel and read books. Thank God those days are behind me.

# Chapter 20

## PREACHING MINISTRY

I ran for and loss both races for City Council of Long Beach in 1984 and 1986. I now wondered what I would do in life. I had a BA Degree and a Juris Doctorate Degree, and I kept wondering what would do I in life. I did not pass the bar to become a lawyer and I couldn't seem to win political office on two tries. I then remembered my dad being a preaching and so I decided to preach like my dad. I felt since nothing else had succeeded in my life, maybe God's intention was for me to preach since all the other professions were blocked so that I could go into the ministry. I also remembered my grandfather Elijah had been the Pastor of two churches and so I went into the ministry. I needed to find my niche in life, and I thought for sure it has to be the ministry.

They say some ministers were sent and some just went. I was in the latter category. My ministry flourish for a brief minute and then evaporated like smoke into thin air. I would never find my niche in life in ministry. Although I went on the radio and watched my church membership grow as high as about 50 people, other ministers would steal my church attendees and others would quit and leave and then my own assistant ministers took people away me and started their own churches.

There is so much evil done under the guise of religion. I remember #$100 came missing out of the tithes and Offerings. I asked the treasurer where the missing money was. He would apparently put his own offering in the plate and then steal it back. I guess he saw taking his own money back as not stealing. I said to him, my question is not who is stealing out of the treasury, but my question is why does the thief only steal from you" He looked at me perplexed and said nothing. He said nothing because he was the thief.

I finally threw in the towel one day. I would find out later in life that my niche was not ministry. I would not find my niche until I started teaching and coaching. I would finally find something that I was actually good at in life when I started teaching and coaching the youth.

I realize now that everything I had been through in life was preparation for me to teach and coach. It was these two professions that I would actually flourish in and win over people and prosper in life. I would buy homes, cars, and travel like I had never done before in life when I started teaching and coaching and left drugs alone.

I would also stop chasing skirts and focus on pleasing one woman and raising great kids. All the things I had done before in life running for office, preaching and teaching in the ministry, would actually help me hone the skills of teaching at colleges and high school and make me an excellent professor and coach that would win basketball championships and track meets along with football games and produce students that would later become lawyers.

I would then begin to read about great scholars and writers and my entire outlook on life would change. I would begin to see a lot of my education had simply being propaganda and I would begin to look at the entire world through a different prism and see life from a totally different perspective. I had finally found my niche and it was not ministry but teaching and coaching.

I have no regrets about starting the Positive Church of Jesus Christ and winning many people over as followers of Christ, but over the years I became disillusioned with the religion, itself, as I begin to ask questions and could not receive answers. I still believe in God, but I am not a fan of organized religion, in any form, at all.

I simply don't believe Jesus was a White Man as is often portrayed by the Media and Europeans. The paint him in books and on film as a European. People often say what difference does it make? I say if it doesn't make any difference in his color then why did they change the complexion of Jesus? It is obvious to me; It was done to support the propaganda of white supremacy and so the world is not bowing down to God but instead they are bowing down to the image of a White man.

I remember before I taught in college that I used to preach in the church and often times I would use humor to deliver my messages. Sometimes, I would deliver a message and the entire church would be laughing and cracking up at my sermon, but there was always one or two people crying or running to the front of the church to declare that they were a sinner.

That paradox amazed me, why were some people laughing, and others convicted and crying at my sermons. I realized later that the message was not intended for those laughing, but instead it was intended for those that were convicted and crying.

I no longer preach, now I just teach at college, and again I still use humor in class and on FB and I have noticed some people laugh at what I say in my posts and classes; but others often get become quite upset, some even angry, and others think, and some even cry today. I am having the same effect with my speech, but yet it is in a quite different forum, but it still reminds me that a particular post is, or speech is, not always for everyone, but it is always for someone.

As I said earlier, I do not believe in Christianity because they painted Jesus as a white man with blond hair and told us in slavery to bow down to him. I believe they have perpetuated a lie on his ethnicity to promote white supremacy. Most of the people in that region of the world were actually brown and black people and I refused to go to a church that promotes white supremacy, directly or indirectly.

I like some things about Islam but I don't like how they treat women. I like some things about Hinduism and Buddhism, but I also think all religions have good qualities and bad qualities, and I have just decided to worship the real and living God and not any particular image of a man as God or any other form of organized religion.

Finally, I also change my outlook on life because I believe a lot of science is correct. God doesn't cause hurricanes nor Earthquakes and so science makes many religions look stupid like those pastors that won't listen to science on the Covid 19 virus or religion claiming the world was flat when it was actually round.

I simply want a relationship with God that makes sense and I don't see it in many religions. Also, people like Jim Jones that convinced 900 Christians to commit suicide and that one church told the men to cut off their balls and wait for a space ship (Heaven's Gate) and then they are teaching people that Rabbits lay eggs for Easter, when they know only Chickens and Reptiles are the ones that lay eggs. It is simply bullshit to me that many follows blindly their religions without even thinking. God would have made us robots if he didn't want us to think.

I think I am an Iconoclast.

However, I recognize each of you have the right to worship God as you see fit. There is a verse in the Bible that says they have a zeal for God but without knowledge. Many people are zealous for God, but they do not really know him. My wife still practices Christianity, but I do not. I still like the verse in the Bible where it says the true worshipper shall worship me in Spirit and Truth but not much else. The rest of it has been used to subjugate women, killed Native Americans in the millions and enslave African- Americans.

Mankind came up with worshipping images. There is also a verse in the Bible that says the true worshippers shall worship me in spirit and truth...... that is where I am! It also says don't make graven images of me in the Bible. The Whites say they can make Graven Images because they are not worshipping them, but the truth is, they are worshipping them or teaching us to worship them.

I was at a hospital once and this man pulled out a picture of a white Jesus and started to pray to the picture. I am learning that God is real and that I do not need a mediator to go directly to him. I am developing an inner peace and an inner determination to succeed in life. I see myself in a Bentley next year. I see more real estate like an apartment complex. I see leaving a big estate for my kids. I see becoming a millionaire.

Also, I do not like that they tell you the only way to get to Heaven is via the white man and all other nonwhite religions are going to hell. More white supremacy and more white brainwashing bullshit. I think if monkeys took over the world. They would tell us that God is a monkey and have all of us bowing down to a monkey. They would even put a monkey on a cross and tell us he died for us.

There is also a verse that says in the Bible that a lazy man comes to poverty, but the black man has worked hard in slavery from sunup and sundown for close to 400 years and yet most of us are still poor. How can people that work so hard in slavery be broke?

They are broke because they were exploited by their masters. They made their masters rich and the slaves were taught to look for their rewards in Heaven. The white people now have everything that was passed down to them from previous generations. Black people, on the other hand, have received nothing from their previous generation, because they were broke, while making their masters wealthy. The only thing our previous generations passed down to us was hope.

I want the wealth that generations of my people have missed out on. I do not want to be poor another day in my life. They were exploited. They were pimped. The pimp gets all the money, but the prostitute does all the work.

They are not poor because they are lazy. They are poor because they were exploited. The rich man that exploited them left his wealth for his kids and the poor man that was exploited had nothing to give his kids.

Imagine this for generation after generation for almost 400 years. One side getting rich and the other side getting poor. The white man today says I did not do bad, it was my father's father that did bad to Blacks. However, he gave his wealth from our exploitation to his kids. It would be like I robbed a bank and gave the money to my daughter. I am the one that violated the law and then die. I died before I could face punishment, but my daughter that receive that robbed money will benefit from receiving the money. The kids did not rob the bank, but they sure benefitted from what their fathers did.

All my life I have been raised a Christian. My dad was a Christian preacher. My grand dad was a Christian pastor and his dad was a Christian. They were all taught the Christian faith.

Now I am no longer a babe in Christ and as I mature in the faith, I have some serious questions:

Why does the oppressors do evil to the oppressed and the

oppressed are taught to turn the other cheek and forgive the evil done to them?

Why are the oppressed taught to obey their masters?

Why are we taught to look for our rewards in Heaven while the oppressor's have their rewards on earth?

Why are we taught money is evil while the rich enjoy all that life has to offer?

Why are we taught to love our enemies?

Why does Christianity favor the oppressors and teach the oppressed only to pray?

Are we so religious in this life that we have become stupid?

Why are other cultures owners of stores and businesses and most of us are merely consumers? Is this by coincidence or design?

# Chapter 21

## TEACHING

I accidently fell into teaching. My goal in life was to be a lawyer, but after several unsuccessful tries and a failed ministry, I decided to teach after one of my church members invited me to come speak to a group of students at her college. The first invitation produced a second invitation and then the Business Department hired me to teach paralegal courses at the college. I had finally found my niche. I now teach Business Law One and Two and other legal courses at the college Level. I stop preaching and I started teaching at the college and then found jobs at other colleges in Los Angles and Covina. I often use humor and logic to teach business law with an emphasis that forces people to think and write for themselves. Many students that I have taught have gone forward in life to become lawyers and several of my former students own their own business.

I also started coaching my kids in track, basketball and football and I actually begin winning contest and games. I went undefeated two years in a row in basketball. I had finally found my niches. I could inspire young people to be victorious. I could read and I read books on every subject. I even asked Coaches that beat me how they had won, and they were eager to share their l knowledge with me. I believe we learn more from defeat than we do from victories in life.

My secret to teaching is telling jokes. I use jokes to amuse the students and hold their interest. Once I get them laughing, I notice that they pay attention to what is being taught. I have been teaching a Business Law Course One and Two for about 15 years and I used the law in a witty sense to convey my message and to explain intentional torts, negligence, strict liability and a host of other topics.

Some of my jokes are risqué and some are clean, but they often reinforce the topic that I am teaching. My students at night say after working all day that they need humor to keep them awake and I try to supply as much as I can. Sometimes they are laughing so loud that you can hear it in the hallway. Several instructors have asked me to keep the noise down.

I often tell the joke about the husband on his dying bed confessing to his wife that he had cheated on her with her sister and mother. The wife replied, "I already knew, that is why I poisoned you, so just relax and accept your fate." It always receives thunderous laughter.

Another Joke I would often tell is a mom told her son that it is time for church and the son replied I don't want to go to church. The mom said you must get up and go to church. The son says give me two reasons that I should go to that church since half the people down there don't like me and the other half I don't like. The mother said well one is you are 35 years old and two is you are the pastor of the church.

Another joke, I often tell is the teacher asked how many Republicans are in her 5th grade class and all the students raised their hands except for one. The teacher asks Suzy, "Why didn't you raise your hand?" Little Suzy says. "Because I am a Democrat. My Mom and Dad are Democrats and my whole family are Democrats." The teacher said, "That is no reason to be a Democrats, if your whole family were thieves, would you be a thief." Little Suzy, said, "No, in that case I would be a Republican"

I also believe in dreams and I believe our subconscious mind is telling a story to our conscious mind. I once dreamed that I had three bikes that were stolen and the very next day I lost three jobs. A man told me to apologize to his daughter for kicking her out of the Jr High School classroom and I refused and the very next week I was let go from one teaching job and two coaching jobs.

This man once told me he had a dream of large dinosaurs swimming in his backyard pool. He later found out that his wife was messing with some men with rather large penises. However, the dream said dinosaurs were swimming in his pool and never mentioned men. It was as if his subconscious mind was trying to warn him, she was cheating on him. You figure out the rest.

Later in my life, a rather narrow minded and closed-minded school District charged me with sexual harassment of a romantic nature. I had never heard of sexual harassment of a romantic nature. They said I had asked a married woman to go to a basketball game with her. I fought it and won. The Judge also ruled in my favor. The school paid me thousands to settle the case. However, the State of California still gave me a reprimand for what they said was the immoral act of asking a married woman to go to a basketball game. A charge I vehemently denied, in vain. I sued in court and won my case.

My favorite sermon when I was preaching back in the days was Moses was learned in all the wisdom of the Egyptians and he was mighty in words and deed. In other words, he walked the walk and talked the talk.

In short, Moses had a good education. Like Moses, everyone should obtain a good education and learn everything there is to know in this life and about this journey. If you think education is expensive than try ignorance. It pays to go to school and it also pays to be self-taught. We can teach ourselves with the vast knowledge available today on the Internet. There is a myriad of subjects that we can learned about on the internet, from foreign languages, history, math, religion, politics, investments, and science, just to name a few!

Learn all you can, while you can, because you are going to need it in this life as well as the afterlife!

It is not only the strong that survive in life, but also the smart and wise!

I also tell my students that they have the right to make a citizen's arrest if they ever witnessed a breach of the peace done in their presence or if they reasonably believed a felony had occurred. I have said," For example, if you are at a party and someone pulls out a bag of cocaine, then you can make a citizen's arrest. "

They always l start laughing.

I love teaching and I can actually motivate students to make sure their reach exceeds their grasp as said by Robert Browning.

# Chapter 22

## COACHING

I also got into coaching by accident. A Lady asked me if I wanted to coach an NJB basketball team for team when I went to sign up my preteen son, Hudena Jr, for basketball. I had never coached a team before, and I was a poor basketball player in my youth. I said No because I had never made the Junior High or High School Basketball Teams. I was not a good player and I had never coached. The lady said, "It does not matter." She overcame my resistance with her persistence. I finally accepted the challenge and went to the library and read every book that they had on basketball. I read books by Magic Johnson, Larry Bird, and John Wooden. I went to coaches that beat me during games as well as other coaches that knew a lot about basketball and picked their brains.

I wasn't a good basketball player, but I was a great coach. A young adult ran upon me one day and I thought for sure he was going to "rob" me when suddenly he said, "Hi Coach James, you coached me in basketball when I was a kid and I just want to say thank you."

I have been a coach for track, football, and Basketball. I won an NJB Championship for Jurupa Valley and also the Moreno Valley Championship. My basic play in basketball was called house and I told the preteens that you must always protect your house and we went two seasons of being undefeated in basketball. I always told my athletes that we are only as strong as our weakest link and they used that mantra to make each other better.

I think we learn more from constructive criticism than compliments. The first year I went 5 wins and 5 losses. The second and third year I won all my games. And I was undefeated with 13-0 seasons. In football, I won all my games in the regular season but lost the final game. It was as if the other coaches knew all my plays in the final and we loss.

You never know how and what you do for others that can turn around and bless you and them and I am so glad that I took time in my life to give back to the community back in the days.

One of the people I admired in life was Ron Alice, he was one of the best track coaches that I had ever meet in my life. He would lead great teams to victory at Long Beach Poly and eventually become the head coach at USC. He was a brilliant man and could get the best out of any of his athletes.

He was also my cross-country coach and under him I ran the 2 miles in a time of 10:30 seconds. He eventually had me run the 600 and I won and then he had me run on the 4x400 yard relay and the 800-yard races. He made me practice with an awesome athlete called Elvie Howard and we competed fiercely against each other in practice, but I could never beat him in practice nor in the track meet. He became just as fast as his opponent in order to win a race. I watched him beat 800-meter runners that had better times than he had. He would simply rise to the occasion and in the heat of the race beat his opponent.

I thought for sure he would win the CIF Championship in the 800 meters, but he tripped during the middle of the race. He was one of the most phenomenal athletes that I have meet in my life.

We also had other great athletes on the team like High Jumper, Carl Miles, Long Jumper, Tony Brown, and the outstanding 4x 100 relay team of James Warren, Leonard Ross, Ricky Ivy and Tony Brown, along with the great Hurdler James Royal and Shot putter Maurice Valentine, just to name a few

I really loved coaching track in my latter years and was able to watch my nephew, Joshua, set an Arcadia track Record in the 60-meter Hurdles.

I am so glad I took the time out of my busy schedule in life to coach these young teenagers on a voluntary basis back in the days. I also coached at two high schools in track and field as well as YMCA football and several different basketball leagues in Riverside and Moreno Valley and actually won two championships and had two 13-0 undefeated season records.

Another time I was at a WinCo Grocery Store and a young adult yelled, "Coach James ", and ran up to me and thanked me for my coaching days and even recently coming out of the Cleaners an old athlete saw me and gave me praise for coaching him and told me he was married now and had graduated from college.

We ran some of the fastest time at Jurupa Valley High School when I was coaching the track team. Coach Green hired me to assist him in training the sprinters and my son, Jamaal, ran a 48 in the 400-meter. Ray ran a 10.9 in the 100-meter dash and Nick Hill, Jamaal James, Steve Young, Ray Blackburn, Kendall Edwards, set a new record in the 400 meters relays and 1600 relay meters.

I was amazed that I had trained such great athletes.

I really enjoyed coaching athletes in track and in 1998 our athletes at Jurupa Valley High school we won the 100-meter dash and 200-meter dash with Ray and then we won the 400-meter relay with Steve, Kendall, Jamaal and Ray. We also won the

400-meter dash with Jamaal and then the 4x 400 relay with Nick, Jamaal, Steve, and Ray. We won 5 of the 10 track Running events. Ray and Jamaal were simply phenomenal that day in the District Wide Championship and all of our strenuous training had benefitted us as a team.

I also love taking my son Hudena James to the championship in Basketball twice at a league in Moreno Valley and another league in Riverside. The first victory was against an undefeated team in Moreno Valley. We slowed down their fast break and beat them with outside shooting from my son and his teammates. The next year my son played for Moreno Valley and we defeated other formidable Moreno Valley Teams in order to win the championship. I had found my niche and it was coaching young athletes.

I also took my daughter JV Basketball Team at Jurupa Valley to go play Chino Hills. The Coach of Jurupa Valley was shocked when I came back and told him we had defeated the Chino team. I will never forget the look on his face as I told him we had won.

# Chapter 23

## HOUSES

We bought a house, loss a house, bought a house and sold it for a profit and then bought a third house. My life has been like the letter W. It seems to go up and down in the old days but now it is actually stable.

We spent the early years of our marriage living in apartments. My wife had been bugging me to buy a house, but I didn't think we were ready. I looked at houses in Long Beach and the only house I could afford you had to bend your back in order to enter the home. We finally decided to leave Long Beach and move to Riverside.

In 1990 I bought my first house for $170,000, 7 years later 1997 I lost that same house in foreclosure. I found out later that Mortgagee resold the house for $140,000. Now, fast forward 18 years later and I would sell another house and made $140,000 profit. Now I am living in a new home for $354,000 and I tend to sell that for $500,000 in a few years. My goal in life is to retire and write books and flip houses,

It seems like we buy a house every 13 years. We bought our first house in 1990 and loss it to foreclosure in 1997. We bought our second house in 2003 and sold it later for a profit in 2015.

We moved into our newest and biggest 6 bedroom and 3-bathroom house in 2016. All I can say is never give up, never quit, and never stop hustling and learning from your mistakes and please live well.

My dad bought his first house in the 1960's for $28,000 in Long Beach, California. People at that time thought $28,000 was a lot of money for a house. Today we would spend $500,000 or more for that same house in Long Beach.

Whenever I am in Long Beach, I drive by the house that I was raised in on the westside at 2701 Caspian. I do not bother the occupants of the home, but I simply sit there in my car and reflect on all the memories I had there as a youngster.

I couldn't afford to buy a house in Long Beach in the 1980's, so we moved and bought our first house in 1990 in Riverside, California for $170,000. We loss it in 1997 to a foreclosure. My son told me the other day that the house we loss is now worth $500, 000.

I bought another house in 2001 and paid about $100,000 for that house and I later sold it for a tremendous profit of more than $140,000.

I am telling people this fact in order to urge you to buy real estate property, because although it fluctuates, it is always a good investment.

In fact, the new house we have now lived in for the last 4 years already has over $150,000 in equity.

People tell me there is no difference in renting and buying a home, but I disagree

All of the increased value of your home is called equity. So, if you owe a mortgagee or creditor $200,000 on a house and the house increased in value to $300,000 then that extra $100,000 belongs to you.

My grandmother Rozelle own a three-unit apartment

complex and she used the rental money from her tenants to pay her mortgages.

Please talk to a real estate agent! Buying a house was the best decision we ever made in life.

# Chapter 24

## Cops and In-laws

I watched the George Floyd Murder on television. He was the Black man choke to death by the knee of a white police officer in Minneapolis, Minnesota during Covid 19 stay at home orders. His death resulted in protests and even riots all over the world and people shouted even louder than ever that- Black Lives Matter and "I cannot breathe." While some people say all lives matter, the fact remains that all lives are not on fire. The urgency is to put out the fire on Black Lives. Donald Trump seek to silence the protestors and not the injustices that cause the protests. If they take away the injustices, then the protests would stop.

During the midst of all these protests, I realized that I was surrounded by cops in my wife's family. My wife's family consisted of Queen Esther and Robert. My wife and I both have dads named Robert. My wife had a family of 7 kids. They consist of my wife, Jackie, who is the oldest followed by Robert, Lynn, Renee, Nancy, Melvin, and Kelvin. 3 of her brothers were Sheriff or LAPD and her dad was a LAPD Officer that was shot in the Watts riots. My own son followed his granddad and became a LAPD officer. He has since resigned and gone into computers and his own trucking business. My wife's dad and I were always arguing about police brutality in a respectable fashion. His favorite line was if you want to be treated like a king then come to Los Angeles and the LAPD will treat you like a King-Rodney King. I would argue against police abuse and he would often claim it was not abuse. We were both biased in our perspective.

My sister in laws are all one of a kind. My sister in law Nancy is always ready to fight. My kids said she was going to beat up a grown man for how he was treating our kids. One time she was on the phone complaining to my wife and my wife said did your husband hit you. She said, and I repeat, "Hell no, he knows better than to do that" and we all laughed. She was at a basketball game and she didn't like the way the referee was calling the game against her daughter Queena. She walked on the court to give the Referee a piece of her mind and threw Mercedes's baby to me to catch like a football. They apparently told the Referee that their lawyers were there, referring to me, but my son, Hudena Jr and I got up and left. The game I thought they were going to turn the place out.

Another sister Renee is very business orientated and runs her own day care center. One of my cousin Rodney came over my house for a party and he was playing the dozen against me and telling me that I wasn't this and I wasn't that. Renee, Marion, and Nancy, who all play the dozen well came to my defense. They talked about Rodney so bad that he shut up for the rest of the evening. Renee is very quick-witted and thinks fast on her feet. She would have been a great lawyer My last sister in law is Marion. Her high school sweetheart waited until they meet again in their 50's and married her. Some of you thinking about throwing in the towel on marriage should actually take note. Marion does a lot of interpretation of dreams and is deeply religious. She is just like my wife Jackie and doesn't drink alcohol at all.

I would often go on to speak out against police brutality

before the city council of Long Beach back in the days. They even showed me on the national television NBC news speaking out against police brutality when a black man named Don Jackson was thrown through a plate Glass window of a business in Long Beach. I protested how Blacks were treated by the Long Beach Police before the Long Beach City Council and they harassed me for days by giving me tickets for trivia matters in Long Beach.

Another time, I was in North Long Beach talking to some friends in a car after 12 midnight and two police drove up and shouted, "WHAT ARE YOU BOYS DOING OUT HERE AT THIS TIME OF NIGHT?" I said. "I am a law school student, and I cannot believe you actually talk to people in that manner" The two cops rapidly rolled up the window drove off. One of the cops had a woman that looked like a prostitute in the backseat of the car. My friends in the car said, "From now on I am going to use that line" and we all laughed.

Robert was my wife oldest brother. He was extraordinarily strong and could run really fast. He also won weightlifting contest. He told me he was one of the kids watching me when I had fights at Silverado back in my younger days. I fought Arthur as a teenager at Silverado. Little did I know my future brother in law was watching me fight.

Robert, my brother in law, would later threaten to beat me up once he found out that one of his other sisters was being beat up by her husband. He was shocked to learn his sister had been beat on by her by husband. He asked me, at a picnic, "Did I also beat on my wife." I jokingly said, "I beat her all the time". He rushed toward me to attack me, but I told him, "If you hit me then I will own everything you have by tomorrow." After hearing those words, he stopped in his tracks. My wife then told him. "That I never hit on her and that I was just joking" but here is another classic example of my words getting me in trouble and also saving me from a fight.

My wife then went over to talk to him and assured him that I had never hit her. We would later become awfully close and he would visit my house to watch the Superbowl and then weeks later die while his car was stopped at a stop light. He was only 48 years old. He told me he had high blood pressure the last time that I saw him and that he had been hospitalized, but his sudden death actually devastated the family. His dad, Robert, sat next to me at the funeral and kept saying, "Parents are not supposed to bury their kids, but kids are supposed to bury their parents" and years later he would die.

My other brother in law was married but divorced his wife and left her to have babies with several different women. He would take care of all of his off springs and become a genius at real estate. One time, as we left a comedy concert, I saw his woman in line with another man. I asked her where her boyfriend was, my brother in law, she said he was parking the car. I said. "We will wait for him because I want to say hi to him." The guy with her appeared nervous and she never introduced him to us. We waited about ten minute and my brother in law never showed up, so we left. Later, I asked my brother in law, "Did he enjoy the comedy concert?" He said, "What concert?" I need to leave that alone!

Both of my brother in laws are smart when it comes to real estate, they have invested well in real property and one of them is actually a real estate broker.

The family on my wife side gets together for picnic and family gathering and does business with each other quite frequently. They are remarkably close knit and look out for each other. Many of them have birthdates on the same days as other family members but in different years.

I have had many encounters with cops outside of my family. A Cop ticketed me in Compton for Jaywalking across the street.

Another cop in Long Beach gave me a ticket when I was trying to tell an old friend to stop prostituting. The cop said I was soliciting. I explained she was my friend and I was trying to get her to stop prostituting and he still wrote me a ticket. In Riverside I ran a red light and the cop asked for my license. He asked me, "Why I ran the red light?" I said. "Have you ever seen the movie Cool Hand Luke?" and he said, "NO". I said. "These two guys escaped from prison and when they are captured and asked why they escaped, they replied it seemed like a good idea at the time, and when I ran that red light it seemed like a good idea at the time." The cop actually laughed and let me go without writing a ticket.

Another time I had an encounter with a military cop that dated my girlfriend Marcella while I was visiting my girlfriend in Long Beach in my Army days. He wanted to go out some more with her and she didn't want to see him again because her man was back at the fort. He pulled me over several times and threatened to write me a ticket for some bogus reasons. My girlfriend finally told me she had gone out on a date with him while I was away and that is why he was harassing me, I wrote a letter to his supervisors and he never bothered either of us again.

Today, I put both my hands out whenever the Moreno Valley Police pull me over. One cop said that is not necessary. I said. "You shoot at black targets in training and I am black" and he started laughing.

I have had many encounters with the police. One of my scariest moment was in 1974 when a policeman pulled me over in St. Louis on my way to see the Exorcist movie with Linda Blair. Sitting in the passenger seat was a white girl named Kathy and I thought the cop was going to stick it to me, but he didn't. He was awfully polite and respectful and told us to enjoy the movie. My worst fears were placated by his kindness and he didn't even write me a ticket. What really scared me was that movie when Linda

Blair's head turn around, I literally jumped out of my seat.

On another occasion, I was in El Dorado Park in Long Beach, parked inside the park, near a bunch of a trees, late at night, and this woman with me had a warrant for her arrest. I had a gun under the seat. Two cops suddenly and abruptly pulled up behind us and I immediately got out of the car and asked what the problem. He said, "Your license plates have expired." I told him, "I am in Law School and the studies were so overwhelming that registering the car had become an oversight." The officer said, "He had thought about going to law school and that I should apply for a job with the District Attorney Office once I graduated." The other officer said. "Pat him down" but the officer I was talking to said. "We don't need to pat him down; he is a law student." He told me to get that license plate taken care of and they both left. I am so glad they did not check inside that car or ask that woman for her identification. We both would have been arrested that night.

We all got together with the cops in our family and started a family business and everyone contributed money, some more than others One of my former students called me threatening suicide, I told my wife and she suggested we give him a job in our new family business and he sabotaged the entire business We stared a hot dog stand that was very successful but when we acted as independent contractor for a mail delivery services my former student tried to steal the business for himself and did a coup d'état against all of us. I eventually took my money back and got out of the family business.

I went to jail for being behind in child support. My ex-wife wouldn't let me see my son and I wouldn't pay support. It seems childish now, but it was real serious back in those days.

As they were processing us into the Los Angeles County Jail, a white guy was bragging on how it had got several hundred dollars pass the system. The system was the process you went through before going into jail. They take off all your clothes, search all your orifices, and water you down with a water hose as a group. They then take a rubber glove and stick one finger in your anus to make sure you are not sneaking something in. This white guy has obviously gone through all of those processes and still had his money. A few minutes later, he yelled someone had stolen his money. Such is life in County Jail.

The county jail was running by the Los Angeles County Sheriff and they didn't play. A guy told me that criminal didn't run when they saw LAPD, but the y definitely ran when they saw LA Sheriff. They had a bad reputation.

While I was in there, I also met a preacher that had a robbed a store and various other types of criminals. I told the preacher that he didn't have much faith. Most of the inmates were there for drug related charges, mostly blacks and Latino with a few sprinkles of Asians and Whites. I was only in there for 30 days, but it was a rough thirty days. I refused to eat the food and only drunk the milk and juices. People were always begging for my food and I gladly gave it away.

My wife and kids, Jamaal, and Mercedes, came to visit me in County Jail and Mercedes was laughing at my prison attire. Little did she know at that time that one day she would become a correctional officer.

The first day I was in jail, they were processing a large circle of about 50 of us as we sat on the floor for our turn to be processed. These black guys in the circle were staring at me and shaking their head and whispering to each other. I anticipated that some of them were going to jump me. They just kept staring at me. I was now in jail with no mama to protect me. This time I would actually have to fight on my own.

After about 10 minutes of this tension, a black guy said to me some guys wanted to beat you up. They said you were an undercover cop, but I told them you were cool. I wasn't a cop, but I did work for the City Attorney's Office in Compton. Those words - I told them you were cool were refreshing to my ears. His mere words had saved me from a beat down- you are cool.

Wow! No beat down today.

The other thing I remember is there were 4 beds to a cell. 2 upper bunkbed and 2 lower bunkbeds. I came to my cell one day and a lower bunk bed guy had taken my upper bed bunk. I said you need to get off my top bunkbed. He said he was a gangster and announced his gang affiliation. I said I don't give a fuck about you or your gang, you better unass my bed. He got down after my demand. I think jail bring out the worse in you. I actually would have fought him over that bed.

The guards didn't like me because I constantly wrote letters to the Judge via my wife about the mistreatment I received from the guards. When it came down to release me, they close my cell and opened it again playing games with my release. I vowed never to see that place again and I never did.

Also, one time, this black guy asked this white boy to get off his bed. The white guy said, "Make me." I said, "Didn't you hear him say to get the fuck off his bed, then get the fuck off his bed." The white guy got up and left. The black guy said, "Thank you." I couldn't believe I was as acting like that in jail, but that definitely was my alter ego.

# Chapter 25

## GALLANTRY AND FAVORITE QUOTES, MEMORIES, AND JOKES

I would have done well in the days of Knights and Damsels in distress. I have chased after a purse snatcher twice and both times they dropped the purses and a bike snatcher once and he dropped the bike. I also walked a fearful and battered woman from the courthouse to her car once.

Many men will fight a woman and yet run for a gun when it comes to fighting a man. I found that quite interesting. The particulars are that I just left the family law court in Riverside and this woman was afraid to go outside the courthouse because her husband was outside waiting to beat her up and I told her that I would walk her outside the courthouse to her car. She was turning her head left and right as frightened as a Deer. I am glad he did not show up and she probably is also. I think I need to update my will. This male gallantry of mine may be costly in this violent age of society where some men simply love beating up women.

My son reminded me this morning that a grown man stole a 12 year old's white kid's bike and I jumped in my car and chased him down and made him get off and took the bike and gave the bike back to the kid. He repeatedly thanked me profusely.

I once saw this guy snatch a woman's purse in front of a church. I chased after him until he dropped the purse. What was I thinking in those days?

I also chased after purse snatchers twice and made them drop the purses. I actually think I was "stir fry crazy" when I was younger!

They say God watches over fools and babies

Don't be anyone's fool.... Don't let people piss on you and tell you that it is raining. Stay wise and sharp in all that you do in life. Remember that the world is full of fools.

I am sitting here today and thinking about some of the crazy things that I did when I was younger.

Thank God for his protecting fools and babies. I would not do any of those things today. Have you ever done anything foolish or crazy in your own life?

Here are some of my favorite quotes, memories, and jokes:

Always remember that we have two minds and the "critical mind" will always discourage you while the "creative mind" will encourage you. The critical mind exists to create doubt and discouragement, but you, like I, will not listen to him or her. May all your dreams come true and remember your best days are always in front of you but stop listening to the critical and discouraging mind!

I remember my son and daughter were about 10 and 8 years old and my wife and I came back from shopping and we smelled the scent of cooked food in the house. We had told them to stay out of the kitchen, but they decided in our absence to try to cook pancakes and eggs. They adamantly denied they had done anything wrong. I checked the pots and pans and they were still wet from recently being washed. They had cleaned up well but failed to remove the scent from the air. They were caught! We laugh about it now that they are adults, but it was not funny back then. ;)))

Have you guys ever thought about the fact that in a sense we are similar in nature to tamed horses and yet we were formerly wild horses.

We say we are free but isn't the wild horse the one that is truly free to roam and go as he or she pleases in life. We are more like the animals in the zoo than the animals in the wild. We have been taught religion, educated, directed, guided, corrected, trained, socialized, and taught not to behave like our former selves. We are essentially now civilized human beings; we suppress the thoughts of the id and deny the existence of the pre-conscious mind, yet we run to the zoo to see animals caged, travel to Africa to see animals in the wild, run to the ocean for the calmness and peace and yet all the time we wonder are we tamed or not. I, for one, cannot resist going to the beach, not to swim, but simply to watch the waves come in and out and wondering about the beginning of mankind. There is simply more to us humans than we will ever know in a lifetime!

This is a tragedy that I thought was a comedy:

I really had a good laugh today. This female client was telling me about how two boyfriends, one invited and the other not, came to her house at the same time. Her female roommate apparently answered the door and let both into the living room. She then went into the bedroom and told my client that "her men" were in the living room waiting for her and started laughing. My client then went in the living room and asked both men would they like something to drink and fixed them both a glass of wine. (I can just sense the tension in the room as she is telling me the story)

As she is telling me the story, I am laughing really hard and can't believe how in the midst of this madness she is actually acting so calm. She goes on to tell me that the two men are eyeing each other, eyeing her, and sensing that they are not at ease, she goes to her roommate and asked her to keep one of them company, an offer which she refused, as her roommate continues to laugh. My client then goes back into the living room and tries to start a conversation with them both. Finally, one of the men finishes his drink and abruptly gets up and leaves.

She then yells at the other man for coming by uninvited, asked him to leave, and called on the phone to the man that left abruptly to come back. He refuses to come back and instead invites her to go over to his house and she told me that the inevitable occurred when she went to his house - they made love. As she was telling me the story, and in between laughing, I said to myself the guy that left first probably thought he was the loser in this scenario and the guy that stayed was the winner. But in reality, the winner was the guy that left and refused to put up with this madness.

As she was telling the story I could imagine the tension in the room, laughter from her roommate, and then how calm and collected she was in the midst of the madness. The person I admired the most was the guy that got up and walked away. She told me that the guy that walked away is still her man!! Wow!

Anyway, I thought it was a funny story and her name shall forever remain anonymous!!

Is this true? I am just asking for a friend.

Which one is the quickest way of spreading a rumor (or gossip) in life?

Pick a selection:

A: Telegram  
B: Telephone  
C: Text  
D. Tell a woman

I just want to take a moment to complain right now, everyone is complaining these days, so here are my litany of complaints:

I only have two cars right now, where is my third car and what is taking it so long to get here?

My refrigerator is full, but where is my "freezer "and what is taking it so long to get here!

I have $200 in my pocket right now, but I need $300.

Life is just so terrible these days; I mean all my kids are healthy, strong, and wise; but I just want them to be healthier, stronger, and wiser.

I live in a nice two-story house, but I want a bigger house with servants, like a butler, chauffeur and a maid.

My life is just terrible these days and I wish I had more of everything. I only have three dogs and I know people that have four. I also wished that I had a boat and a plane.

I, and others, are so busy looking at what we don't have sometimes that we don't appreciate what we already do have in our lives. :))))

I went to the park to shoot some hoops (Basketball). As I approached the basketball courts, I saw Afro American and a Mexican American squabbling with each other and throwing punches for a few second and then backing up and then returning to throwing punches. I asked everyone gathered around them why were they fighting, and everyone said I do not know, while others shouted fight, fight! So, I walked up the Afro -American fighting the break in fighting, and said why are you fighting? He said something to the effect that the Mexican American had dissed him. I said you guys have been standing here for a good 30-minute fighting, someone has called the police and you are going to go to jail for bullshit. I said I am a minister and I am also into the law and too many brothers are going to jail and getting a criminal record for nothing. I said you need to get out of here now. He went and grabbed his jacket and left. I then went to the Mexican American and said the police are probably on their way and you are going to go to jail for bullshit. You need to go to the other side of the park and disappear. You have a baby and he deserved to see you not in jail. He left as well. As I left and the crowd left, I was reminded of Jesus verse where he said blessed are the peacemaker. My wife and son said I should not have done it, but it is done! How was your day?

Make sure you travel in life and experience other cultures. There is more to life than our neighborhood.

Everyone has critics. If you say I am going right, someone will always say you should of went left. If you go North, someone will say you should of went South. If you give the right answer to a question, someone will say you took too long, or you had ulterior motives.

If you die early, someone will say that you were robbed of your life, but if you live a long life, then someone will say when are you ever going to die!

Don't live to please your critics. Just live life to its fullest, pursue your dreams and do what you know is right in your heart and respect every man and woman on this earth with love!!Remember no man or woman in history has ever been able to please everyone and if you try than you will be engaging in an exercise in futility! Enjoy your life, it is a gift from God and what you do with it is your gift to him! Live well!

They say the bigger the aquarium you put a Goldfish fish in than the bigger the Goldfish.

In short, Goldfish stay small when they are in a small aquarium and yet the same Goldfish will grow bigger in a big aquarium or a lake.

Couples keep rowing in same direction.... many couples row against each other and never progress.

Moses was learned in all the wisdom of the Egyptians and he was mighty in words and deed. In other words, he walked the walk and talked the talk.

In short, Moses had a good education. Like Moses, everyone should obtain a good education and learn everything there is to know in this life and about this journey. If you think education is expensive than try ignorance. It pays to go to school and it also pays to be self-taught. We can teach ourselves with the vast knowledge available today on the internet. There is a myriad of subjects that we can learned about on the internet, from foreign languages, history, math, religion, politics, investments, and science, just to name a few!

Learn all you can, while you can, because you are going to need it in this life as well as the afterlife!

It is not only the strong that survive in life, but also the smart and wise!

We often do not listen to our subconscious mind even though it is often speaking to us in dreams and visions. Our subconscious mind sees and knows things that we do not know on a conscious level.

Our subconscious mind often speaks to us figuratively rather than literally and it often perplexes us and even has to disguise the message in order to actually get it upstairs to the conscious mind.

Here is an example, a friend of mine told me he had a dream that dinosaurs were swimming in his backyard pool. Years later, he found out his wife was cheating on him. His subconscious mind was trying to tell him years before with the illustration of the dinosaurs and pool but his conscious mind simply didn't want to believe it because he trusted his wife.

Our subconscious mind is always speaking to us and sending us disguised and distinct messages, whether our conscious mind accepts it or not!

Our conscious mind often rejects messages from the subconscious.

I once gave an adult person a $2 bill and I told that person to hold on to this $2 bill until I ask you for it, and if you have it on you at that time, then I will give you a $100 dollar bill. I said it might be a month or two month or even three months before I ask you; but when I ask you for it, then you need to pull it out.

One day, a month later, I asked the person to see the $2 bill and they said that they had spent it. WOW!!!

A If they made all women wear chastity belts today, then most man in this world would be taking classes on how to become a locksmith

You obviously have me confused with someone who cares!

If I had your money, I would burn mine.

People are taking the stairs to Heaven but sliding on a slide to hell.

An eagle never flies down and fights with a barking dog.

Trust your Instincts

A bumblebee flew into college and the professor explained to him that it is impossible for bumblebees to fly because their body weight is too large for their small wingspan. The bumblebee walked out of class and never flew again.

Many of us are like that bumblebee in life, even though God has gifted us to do the fly, many of us will listen to others tell us that we can't do and simply give up.

A dog is so smart that his master decides to send him to college.Home for vacation, his master asks him how college is going."Well," says the dog, "I'm not doing too great in science and math, but I have made a lot of progress in foreign languages.""Really!" says the master. "Say something in a foreign language."

The dog says, "Meow!"

We all meet on this internet at a synchronistic time and we find people in different stages of their respective lives and some are of course very happy, and some are, without a doubt - simply miserable.

Some of us are having babies and others are having abortions. Some of us are shouting out our new jobs and others are losing theirs's. Some of us welcome the arrival of a new baby and some of us are saying bye to departed loved ones. Some of us have lost romantic love and some of have just found the love of our life. Some of us have graduated from school and others have dropped out. Some are buying clothes and purses, and some are homeless. Some just bought a new car and someone had theirs's repossessed.

Yet at this moment, at this time, and on this day, we meet again on FB.

I hope all is well on your end, but it's just possible that it may not be. Although, I am in a fairly good mood most of the time, you just might be bitter right now or even anal retentive.

When you are talking to someone on Fb, remember this may not be their best day or it just may be the best day of their life!!

Stay Up, Look Up, Get Up and Stay Up!

A white guy is at an ATM; two black guys come to rob him and demand his ATM card and to know the password to his account. He refuses to divulge his password because It is the "N" word.

He explains to them that I can't tell you my password because if I do this robbery may just turn into a homicide. :))))))

A seven-year old boy was at the center of a Dallas, Texas courtroom drama yesterday when he challenged a court ruling over who should have custody of him. The boy has a history of being beaten by his parents and the judge initially awarded custody to his aunt, in keeping with child custody law and regulation requiring that family unity be maintained to the highest degree possible.

The boy surprised the court when he proclaimed that his aunt beat him more than his parents and he adamantly refused to live with her. When the judge then suggested that he live with his grandparents, the boy cried and said that they also beat him.

After considering the remainder of the immediate family and learning that domestic violence was apparently a way of life among them, the judge took the unprecedented step of allowing the boy to propose who should have custody of him.

After two recesses to check legal references and confer with the Child Welfare officials, the judge granted temporary custody to the "Dallas Cowboys", whom the boy firmly believes are not capable of beating anyone.

An Eagle never fights with a barking dog. Remember always that an Eagle simply does not fly down and fight with a barking dog. The Eagle stays focused on flying and soaring! The dog barks at the Eagle because he or she wishes that they could fly like an Eagle.

Never jump over a dollar to get to a dime but definitely jump over a dime to ger t to a dollar

Water kills a chicken trying to swim but it is no problem for a duck

# EPILOGUE

Despite what I have been through in life; today, I am a very moral person that plays Golf two and three times a week. I stay on FB two hours a day communicating with friends and acquaintances throughout the day and I am enjoying the gradual aging process. I also enjoy watching my adult kids making parenting decisions. I love spending time with grandkids and watching them excel in academics and sports right before my very eyes.

I plan on teaching Business Law a few more years on the college level and then retiring just to write about life and people. I love traveling and visiting new places with my wife of over 40 years and I have enjoying reminiscing about my past memories of old in this book and I cannot wait to write about new experiences. I feel my life has been interesting, despites the ups and down, I have survived, and I am here to enjoy another day. Thank God

I plan to spend the last years of my life flipping houses and writing books. I hope you enjoyed this book. Stay up and wise.

CPSIA information can be obtained
at www.ICGtesting.com
Printed in the USA
LVHW041153171120
671900LV00005B/334